WHAT READERS ARE SAYING ABOUT THE JEANNIE LOOMIS NOVELS:

These books are thrilling from beginning to end. It was like Triple Frontier meets Tomb Raider crossed with Indiana Jones. Under the guise of American playboys, a group of Gulf War veterans known as the Banshees, join with a biblical historian, Nancy Harding, embarking on a heist to track down and steal the Ark of the Covenant. I loved the interwoven historical details, the lust and the fast pace of the story. An absolute page-turner that is well-researched, well-written and edited, and an awesome read for anyone who enjoys thrills and action!

Amazon Rating

The author weaves two story lines together-both taking place in the Bay area. The central character is a female agent. She is strong and likeable without being a cartoonish, super-hero type. There is a strong conservative political aspect to the author's writing. If this doesn't bother you, you will enjoy a well-told tale.

★★★★★

Amazon Rating

These are well-written thrillers. The author does a fine job of combining 2 unrelated coincidental events making them and the characters interact realistically. Using 9-11 as a backdrop is always risky, but it's handled respectfully here.

Amazon Rating

Time Game

Time Game

ISBN: 978-1-7348524-3-1 (hardback)
978-1-7348524-4-8 (paperback)
978-1-7348524-5-5 (ebook)

Printed in the United States of America

Time Game

A Jeannie Loomis Novel

GARY J. ROSE

OTHER BOOKS BY THE AUTHOR:

JEANNIE LOOMIS NOVELS

Ark of the Covenant – Raid on the Church of Our Lady Mary of Zion

Star Chamber

Forgotten Plans

House of Special Purpose

NON-FICTION

Towards the Integration of Police Psychology Techniques to Combat Juvenile Delinquency in K-12 Classrooms.

Hitting Rock Bottom (Amazon bestseller)

How to Create a Public-School Military Style Bootcamp

Teaching Inside the Walls

This book is for my mom,

my daughter, Mike and Mary Lake

and Drs. Fred and Jane Vallier

PROLOGUE

An article in the October 2019 Atlantic magazine stated that as the number of serial killings in the U.S. has supposedly fallen, so too has the rate of solved or "cleared" (detective lingo) murder cases. In 1965 the U.S. homicide clearance rate was 91 percent; by 2017 it had dropped to 61.6 percent, one of the lowest rates in the western world. In other words, about 40 percent of the time murderers get away with murder. Some experts believe that serial killers are responsible for a significant number of these unsolved murders.

Thomas Hargrove, the founder of the Murder Accountability Project--a nonprofit that compiles homicide data--calculated how many unsolved murders are linked by DNA evidence. He believes that at least 2 percent are committed by serial offenders, translating to about 2,100 unidentified serial killers.

Michael Arntfield, retired police detective and author of 12 books on serial murder, thinks the number of active serial killers is closer to three or four thousand. If such estimates are correct, why aren't more killers getting caught?

Professional speculation is that a handful of factors account for this discrepancy: increased expertise (killers study other murderers' mistakes and learn how to fool cops by planting false evidence, etc.), constrained resources (detectives may be less qualified than their predecessors-- thanks to stagnant salaries), growing social isolation (potential victims become more vulnerable), and greater geographic mobility ("dots" become harder to connect).

There are serial killers among us who stay one step ahead of law enforcement. They play the *Time Game.*

TIME GAME

A Jeannie Loomis Novel

An early summer serial killer was on the loose. Crossing the country, he lured in women with his charm--and then struck. His kills were quick, and the savagery he subsequently inflicted on victims' bodies became progressively more ritualistic. He vanished after each attack before the police could catch him, believing time was on his side. He was playing the ***Time Game.***

CHAPTER 1

The "Last Call" bar was a converted pizza joint built in the late 1930's in Marin County. Local Hippies-Turned-Yuppies became carb conscious earlier there than in most communities, and the desire for a high carbohydrate-loaded pizza faded, thus transforming a pizza business into a watering hole. The walls of the bar were covered with pennants and signed jerseys, representing all major league sport clubs in the area. Each wall was dedicated to a particular sport. One wall was dedicated to the San Francisco 49ers and was covered with autographed jerseys of past and present stars, pictures of previously won championships, an overhead picture of their former stadium, Candlestick Park, as well as the new facility in Santa Clara, and a helmet with the famed SF logo.

Other walls displayed similar articles of the San Francisco Giants, Golden State Warriors, San Jose Sharks and their respective championship trophies.

The sit-at bar itself was made of an extremely large piece of highly polished redwood almost 30' in length, with red high-back chairs strategically placed a foot apart.

Local patronage kept the bar financially solvent. This evening a male newcomer with blonde hair reaching the middle of his back added to the normal crowd. He was instantly accepted by the locals after announcing he was buying the next round of their favorite alcoholic beverage.

His attention immediately fell on a 5'6" brunette that entered the bar. Wearing a tan colored silk blouse and black Levis that she appeared to have been poured into, she waved at the crowd who hooted back at her. She walked up to the bar and placed an order with the female bartender. He approached her while she was opening her purse and said this round was on him. She looked at him and smiled, but since she did not recognize him, she was suspicious of his offer. He looked like a stereotypical jock wearing a checked red and black flannel shirt. She thought that it was probably a Pendleton. He had piercing hazel eyes and a full beard and mustache.

"That's OK," she said. "You don't need to buy my drink." "You're hurting my feelings," he said while smiling. "I just bought the last round for everyone." She looked around at the other patrons. One of the locals pointed at the male offering to buy her drink and gave the thumbs up.

"OK, if you insist. My name is Sheila," offering her hand. "Hi, Sheila; my name's Daniel. Nice to meet you." Sheila noticed that Daniel held on to her hand a little longer than normal, but maybe he already had a few, she thought. She did not see a wedding ring, but these days who knows or who cares. "You seem to be in a good mood," he said as they both watched the bartender make a Manhattan for Sheila. "Actually, I am. I just received a promotion at work."

"Wow! Congratulations," he said as he hoisted his beer mug and clanged it against Sheila's drink. "Hey everyone, Sheila got a promotion at work. Drinks for everyone," Daniel shouted to the enjoyment of the locals, many of whom raised their glasses to Sheila.

"Where do you work?" Daniel asked, starting a lengthy conversation that culminated with Sheila joking and flirting with the jock, never asking him what he did for a living.

Sheila excused herself, saying she needed to use the restroom. As she walked toward it, Daniel admired her walk. She was followed into the female section by a slightly overweight middle-aged woman dressed completely in black. Once in the facility she called out to Sheila. "Hey girl. Not only did you get a promotion today, you get hit on by that great looking stud out there."

"Yeah, he's not bad on the eyes is he, and a great personality," Sheila replied.

Sheila returned to her seat next to Daniel. Now comfortable with her new friend, she asked Daniel how much conditioner he went through each week. Laughing, Daniel invited her to a game of pool. The two played a few games and then moved on to darts--initially against each other and then taking on all challengers. As the night wore on, Sheila started to feel the effects of the alcohol since she had not eaten dinner. Several of the locals began leaving. Most thanked Daniel for the drinks on their way out and invited him to return in the future.

"Any chance you could drive me back to my motel?" Daniel asked. "I walked here tonight and I'm a little wasted. It's only a block away." "Not a problem," Sheila said. Only four others were still in the bar as they made their way out. Daniel stopped and gave a sizeable tip to the bartender while winking at her, and the two left.

CHAPTER 2

Special Agent in Charge Lomax was already in his office at the San Francisco FBI bureau sipping his first cup of coffee and watching the news.

"We now go to Jessica Williams who is in Marin County for this breaking news item, Jessica."

"Thank you, Jan. That's right. Police are investigating the body of a young woman found burned in a truck in this Marin County Health Medical Center parking lot in Marin County. Law enforcement personnel have not identified the woman nor supplied much information; although, those who spoke off the record speculate this is possibly the work of serial killer, Daniel Koufax, and victim number seven. That might be a big jump since this pattern doesn't fit his previous murders, but the entire area is in a panic.

Two joggers were returning from this trail along the medical center (pointing in that direction) early this morning, and after rounding that bend saw a fully engulfed older model Chevy pickup in the hospital parking lot. One of the joggers quickly called 9-1-1, and the fire department that responded reported a female body inside. The area's been roped off as a crime scene and being searched by evidence technicians.

As you're aware, beginning in the fall of 2019, a serial killer's been on the loose. Crossing the country, he lures women with his charm and then strikes. Each time he's vanished before the police could catch him. That's it from here. I'll get back to you if I learn any further information. Jessica Williams reporting."

The homicide occurred in Marin County, located in the San Francisco Bay Area across from the Golden Gate Bridge with a population of approximately 250,000. In 2017 its per capita income was $91,000. SAC Lomax knew the area well. San Quentin State Prison is located in the county as well as George Lucas' Skywalker Ranch. Geographically, the county forms a large southward-facing peninsula with the Pacific Ocean to the west, San Pablo and San Francisco Bays to the east, and south across the Golden Gate, the city of San Francisco. Marin County's northern border is adjacent to Sonoma County.

Lomax had far more information on his desk about the burned victim discovery than what had just been shared in the media. Early that morning, units of the Marin County Sheriff's Department and the Marin Fire Department responded to calls about a vehicle fire at the Marin Health Medical Center. One was from a nurse who called 9-1-1. When they arrived, they found a pickup truck burning in the parking lot. Once the flames were extinguished, they found human remains.

The Sheriff's Department contacted their homicide division as well as the coroner and the arson squad. Sheriff's Department homicide detectives Ron Jackson and partner Tony Lucas arrived and were briefed by the uniformed officers at the scene. They were directed to the nurse who had seen the fire start. She said she had arrived for work just before dawn for her early morning shift, and in the parking lot she saw the truck go ablaze. She then faintly saw a man with long blonde hair and full beard running from the truck as the flames erupted, and immediately called the police. She never saw his full face, nor had she ever seen the truck before.

The investigators reported that the fire damage pattern indicated it had been started in the cab and had burned very quickly--probably aided by an accelerant like gasoline, but they would have to wait for a chemical analysis to be positive. The body inside appeared to be female, but it was burned beyond recognition. Some items survived the fire including a backpack holding a purse and a digital camera. Investigators noted that the camera had several photos in its memory. Technicians found several documents in the purse, including a California driver's license for a Sheila Bohls. In private conversations between the two homicide investigators, they assumed this was the work of the serial killer who had already struck three times in their jurisdiction. They had to keep their speculations private so that down the road some smartass defense attorney would not accuse them of focusing on his client prematurely in a rush to judgement.

The truck's plates were run through the DMV, confirming that it belonged to Sheila Bohls with a Marin County address. Further record checks found that she was 31-years old and married to a Steven Bohls. He was contacted and interviewed at home by detectives who suspected he was involved in a domestic homicide, since statistically it is usually the husband who commits the murder. Even though it was too soon for either dental records or DNA to positively identify the female victim, they felt it was Sheila.

Steven Bohls came to the Sheriff's office immediately. Displaying male-pattern baldness a little early for his age which he tried to disguise with a comb-over, he was clean shaven, only 5'7" tall, and probably weighed no more than 150 pounds. Almost immediately, the two veteran homicide investigators started to eliminate him as the primary suspect.

According to Steven, he was home asleep during the time of the arson; however, he had no witnesses that could confirm his alibi. When the detectives showed him items that had survived the truck fire, he positively identified the backpack and digital camera as Sheila's as well as the stored pictures in the camera. Steven could not hold back his tears. As the interview wrapped up, eye contact between the two veteran homicide detectives told each that Steven was not the perpetrator, although they later discussed the possibility that he might have arranged a contract killing. This assumption would require more investigation including bank records and interviews with friends, family, co-workers, and associates. His story had to be corroborated.

Steven stated that the day before his wife's homicide, he had lunch with her at a local Applebee's. He recalled details of their visit including the restaurant and what each had ordered, adding that he and Sheila had been experiencing marital problems and had spent the last couple of nights apart. They talked about reconciling, but things were still strained between them. He said he last saw Sheila around 2 p.m. when they left the restaurant separately, but later, she called him from a local bar called the "Last Call." She was very excited because when she returned to work following their lunch together, she learned that she had received a promotion. Since that call, he had not heard from his wife nor had any idea where she might have gone after leaving the bar.

Detectives Jackson and Lucas followed the direction of the investigation, taking them to the Last Call bar in hopes of interviewing the bartender and anyone else who had been present the night before and might have information about Sheila. This was the first solid lead they had to date. When they arrived, they learned that Monica Bennett had been the bartender. The detectives showed her pictures from the digital camera and she recognized Sheila as a regular. She remembered Sheila arriving late in the afternoon in an extremely good mood since she had learned about a promotion at work--sharing her good news with everyone she came in contact with that afternoon and early evening.

Some customers overheard the discussion at the bar and approached the two detectives. They recalled a man who was talking to her; and although he was not a regular, he had shown up the previous two nights as well. They described him as a large white male with extremely long blond hair well past his shoulders and a full beard and mustache, approximately 6'2" and built like a football player. He called himself Daniel. They believed his last name might be Koufax, but they were not sure. The two detectives quickly glanced at each other. The witness's description seemed to match the description of the man seen fleeing the burning truck--the elusive serial killer.

He seemed interested in Sheila as soon as she entered the bar and he talked to her for quite a while. Daniel was very friendly with everyone and came across as a big spender, buying drinks for Sheila and everyone else in the bar. When the bar closed Daniel asked Sheila for a ride home, saying he lived close by. The bartender said Sheila agreed and the two left together. No one had seen either of them since.

Detective Lucas called Captain Jerry Gilman who was head of the serial killer task force for the San Francisco, Marin County law enforcement agencies, told him they might have identified the suspect: Daniel Koufax. "So, we missed him by what, 12-14 hours?" Gilman asked. "Afraid so," Lucas replied. "This's got to be the luckiest fucker I've ever tried to catch. Time seems to be on his side so far."

Jackson and Lucas showed a photo lineup from the records check to the nurse, bartender, and other individuals who were in the bar the night before. The nurse could only say that the body type seemed to match the individual she saw fleeing the burning truck. The bartender and other witnesses positively identified Daniel Koufax as the person who left the bar with Sheila. "They've got him," both detectives thought. Just like past homicides linked to Koufax, he made no attempt to hide his real identity. Per his ***modus operandi***, he was probably driving the victim's car. Given that possibility, an APB (all-points-bulletin) was issued. Surely, it would only be a matter of time before he was caught.

Daniel Koufax was a white 32-year old male and currently a drifter. He was born in Tennessee and was the only child of Martha and Mario Koufax. His parents died in a residential fire when he was only 13-years old, and having no relatives, he was placed in foster care that bounced him from one foster parent to another.

A day later, Detective Jackson received a phone call from Nathan Gilmore who was the night motel manager of the Cozy Inn not far from the bar where Sheila and Daniel met. He told the detective he was pretty sure that Daniel and Sheila rented a room, judging from the photographs he saw on television that morning.

The detectives secured a search warrant for Koufax's motel room which was only a few minutes away from where the truck had burned. After locating the motel manager, they climbed the stairs to the second floor room door, announced their presence and that they had a search warrant. After several knocks and no answer, the apartment manager handed the key to one of the detectives who allowed two uniformed officers to enter first. Koufax was not inside. It appeared that Koufax had cleared out in a hurry. Their search found a woman's purse containing a wallet that was empty of cash and had no identification. Next to an emptied beer bottle on the coffee table they found a woman's earring. The earring was later shown to Steven Bohls who identified it as Sheila's, having bought it for her several months earlier.

The next day the Marin County coroner conducted Sheila's autopsy with Jackson and Lucas's present. Dental records positively identified the remains as those of Sheila Bohls. She had not burned to death as there was no evidence of fire or soot in her nasal passages; the coroner concluded Sheila had been dead before the fire was started. A mother of three had been killed by manual strangulation. There was no way of determining if semen were present because of the body's condition; there was no sign of sexual penetration. The detectives took their case to the district attorney's office without waiting for a lab analysis of the evidence found on the body. The DA charged Daniel Koufax with murder and issued a warrant for his arrest. The detectives entered everything they had into the NCIC (National Crime Information Center), hoping that one of the 57,000 law enforcement agencies nationwide would catch the killer; but for now, he was still on the loose--probably looking for his next prey.

CHAPTER 3

It was a little after 6 p.m. when Ismail Flores, driving Jeannie's Corvette, drove into the Green Tavern Inn's gravel parking lot in a small town outside Barstow, California. A flashing neon sign advertised that Bud was on tap, and another sign indicated there was also food available. It really was not much of a town; it would probably be called a village in Eastern Europe. Ismail never saw a sign indicating he had entered the town boundaries nor any indication of its population count, but if the Green Tavern Inn was any indication of what the rest of the town looked like, he would not be impressed by a tour. Sporting a designer suit with dark-blue silk shirt and matching tie, Ismail climbed out of the Vette and walked toward the bar entrance.

Before entering, he closed his eyes for a few minutes, allowing his eyes to adjust to the anticipated darkness inside. Upon entering he noticed two locals sitting at the far end of the bar, each nursing a beer. The male bartender, wiping down the bar and aligning bowls of beer nuts, watched as Ismail made his way to the opposite side of the bar.

"How you doing'?" he asked, walking toward Ismail. "Good. I'll have what those two gentlemen are having," Ismail said while nodding in their direction. "Don't know if I would call them gentlemen, came the bartender's reply as he began filling a mug and smiling at the two locals. "Just passing through I assume?" he asked. "Yup, on my way to Big Bear Lake. I have a cabin up there. Just felt I needed some time to myself, and a few days at the lake should do the job."

"I figured as much. Nothing worth seeing in this fucking town, much less staying here. I mean, this is the only place for miles that has any nightlife, and although it's early, won't get much busier than this." He moved a bowl of nuts toward Ismail without saying another word and walked back to the locals. Ismail did a survey of the bar and saw 10 unoccupied booths, a pool table, a dart board, and a card table near the opposite wall.

Halfway through sipping his first beer he noticed a woman coming from the back area of the tavern where the restrooms were located. Her raven hair was pulled into a ponytail and she was wearing what Ismail would describe as Daisy Duke short-shorts. The tails of a red and black checkered blouse were tied over her exposed rock-solid stomach, and the top three buttons of her blouse were strategically opened. She was around 5'5 or 5'6" tall and very thin, and if her complexion were not so flawless, Ismail thought she could be a poster girl for a meth ad. Without hesitation, she walked up the barstool to the right of Ismail, and after saying "hello," sat down. Ismail returned the greeting and reached for a few nuts. Placing her small purse on the bar, she asked if he had a cigarette?

"Sorry, I don't smoke? I thought the entire wacko state of California has outlawed smoking." "Naw, not here. Shit, we can pretty much do whatever we want, huh Jimboy?" she said nodding at the bartender as he walked over to get her order. "I can buy you a drink though," Ismail offered. "What would you like?" "How about a rum and coke?" she said to Jimboy, who was already reaching for a glass. "What brings you to this godless part of the state?" Ismail answered, "As I told Jimboy here, I just stopped to have a drink on my way to Big Bear; I have a cabin up there." "Nice. You must be rich, huh?" she asked and continued without waiting for an answer, "I really like your suit and tie. Is that Gucci?"

"I do alright for myself," Ismail said as he started to play with his wedding ring. "A rich married guy, I see," she said with a big smile showing excellent teeth, while placing her left hand on Ismail right wrist.

"Well, somewhat married."

"What do you mean, somewhat married?" she asked as she began massaging his lower arm and then held his hand.

"You know how it goes. After a while the romance is gone, and it is just two people living under the same roof. What's your name, anyway?"

"I'm Susi. Nice to meet you.....I don't know your name."

"Sorry, I'm Ismail. Nice to meet you Susi."

Her drink arrived having two Maraschino cherries resting on ice cubes at the top. Susi pulled one out by the stem and playfully sucked the cherry back and forth in her mouth while looking at Ismail. Ismail guessed that Susi was maybe the same age as his third daughter, making her around 15-16 years old. The makeup and clothing added on a few years, but there was no way she was 21 or older.

CHAPTER 4

After Susi had two more rum and cokes, they took the Corvette and ended up at a dive motel that Ismail had not seen while coming into town. A few seconds after entering the room reeking of stale cigarette smoke, Suzi jumped on the queen-sized bed, opening the belt buckle of her shorts and the last two buttons of her blouse while pulling it free from the denim cutoffs. She threw the blouse to the other side of the bed showing a black laced push-up bra. Ismail still had his suitcoat on, but had removed his tie and placed it on a small desk.

"What do you think?" Suzi asked as she pushed her breast closer together.

"How old are you anyway, Suzi?" he asked while staring at her breasts still contained in her bra.

"I'm going to be 16 next month," she said, at which point she started to scream while grabbing her bra and covering herself up.

Almost on cue, the motel door flew open and two uniformed officers rushed in, weapons drawn and grabbed Ismail, throwing him to the carpet at the foot of the bed. "On the floor, pervert," the first officer who entered said. Suzi continued to scream and got off the bed while starting to put her blouse on. Once Ismail was cuffed and pulled from the floor, Suzi stopped screaming. "Nice suit. Is that what sugar daddy's wear now-a-days," the second officer asked as Ismail saw him share a wink with Suzi.

"You are in a lot of trouble mister," the first cop said while patting down and removing Ismail's wallet, putting it in his back pocket. "Trying to fuck this young cheerleader. The judge is going to throw the key away once he sees you in his courtroom. Let's go." Both officers grabbed one of Ismail's arms and took him to one of the patrol cars. "Watch your head, child molester," the other cop said as they pushed Ismail into the backseat of the car.

After a brief ride to what appeared to be the outskirts of town, they arrived at a small building adjacent to a volunteer fire department, but separate. A stenciled sign stated "Police Department. Here to serve." Ismail was placed in what one officer called the holding cell, but nothing more than a small 6' by 8' room with an entrance door which had been replaced with bars. "Sit here and shut up, and don't go anywhere," was the command given as the two officers walked down the hallway a short distance before entering another office.

Ten minutes passed before one of the two arresting officers opened the barred door and told Ismail to get up and follow him. Still handcuffed, Ismail walked down the hallway ahead of the officer. They reached the door and the officer pushed it open. Inside Ismail saw another uniformed officer sitting behind a desk displaying gold stars on his collar. On the desk was a wooden carved sign that read "Chief of Police." Along the wall to the right, the second arresting officer with a name plate on his right chest reading "G. Foxworth" watched with a grin on his face.

Ismail saw a seat in front of the desk and sat down. "Who told you, you could sit down?" the chief said while the officer behind Ismail pushed him out of the chair onto the linoleum floor. Ismail struck the floor face down and could taste blood beginning to run from his nose into his mouth. "Stand up, asshole," the other officer said while still leaning on the opposite wall. Ismail struggled but was able to get to his feet on his own. "Against the wall," the chief ordered. "Take off his cuffs. I want to see that watch he's wearing." After the cuffs were removed and Ismail was prone against the wall, his watch was removed and placed on the chief's desk. "Rolex. Presidential model. Nice. Bet that cost you a lot, huh, Mr. Ismail Flores? What are they going for, $30-35,000 dollars? But shit, you dress in designer clothes. Drive a fucken Vette and carry almost a thousand bucks in your wallet. My crack officers learned in a Google search that you are some big shot real estate investor. You got lots of money. Too bad you'll be getting butt fucked in jail for trying to rape 15-year-old Suzi. By the way, how is she?" he asked the two arresting officers. "She's very traumatized chief. When we got there, this perve already had her blouse off and was working on her shorts."

"Take a seat Mr. Flores," the chief said, pointing to the chair in front of the desk.

"That's not true," Ismail said. "She took her blouse off and undid her belt buckle herself, not me."

"Who told you, you could talk?" the chief said as the officer behind him kicked him out of the chair again and onto the floor. "Some perverts are so rude," the chief said while glancing at his officers. "Get back up into your chair before you get the shit kicked out of you. OK, now this is how I see it, Mr. Flores. Judge Sheraton hates child molesters. Shit, if he had his way you would be castrated and then hung, in that order. But instead he'll probably throw the book at you and give you 15-20 years in one of the State of California's outstanding penal institutions.

Now, I don't know if you are aware sir, but even in correctional facilities there is a hierarchy and child molesters are at the bottom of the barrel. Now you're a pretty handsome fellow so you'll probably have your share of romances in prison, whether you want it or not--if you get my drift. If you survive doing your time, you'll not be the same when you get out. Your wife will have taken you to the cleaners. I mean, who wants to be married to a pervert anyway? Your business will be ruined, and to top it all off you'll be labeled a child molester and have to register everywhere you go as what we call, a 290 registrant. Get the picture?"

Ismail did not want another kicking and just nodded, hoping that this form of communication was allowed. "Now, there is another way that me and the boys here could handle this delicate situation you find yourself in. You see, everyone gets horny sometimes, right? Here's what I'm offering you. First, we'll keep the watch; let's say it's worth $25,000 since it's used. You have an American Express card here," the chief said, taking it out of Ismail's wallet. "I want you to transfer another $25,000 to an account I'll write down for you. Now, this here's a promissory note; I know you use it all the time in your business. I have already taken the liberty of writing out my name as well as the sum you'll pay me within seven days. That sum is $100,000."

The chief leaned back in his chair and put his feet on his desk while looking at the two officers. "Now I know what you're thinking. Once we release you, you'll contact American Express, tell them you were robbed and forced to transfer the $25,000. Then, you'll renege on your promissory note and think the situation is over. Well, not too fast. It will get really ugly for you since we'll say that you escaped and we'll issue a manhunt for your ass. Once caught, it'll be your word against little fifteen-year-old Suzi and my two outstanding officers. Get the picture?"

Before he could answer, the nearest officer slapped Ismail in the face, starting his nose bleed again. "The chief asked you a question, prick. Give him an answer."

Before Ismail could say anything, a crashing sound came from the front door area of the station, immediately followed by the sound of individuals running down the hallway toward the office door which suddenly opened.

"What the fuck is this?" the chief said as Jeannie, and three other FBI agents wearing windbreakers entered the room with weapons drawn. "FBI! Put your hands in the air. You three so-called officers of the law are under arrest," Special Agent Jeannie Loomis forcefully announced. "Chief, you should know the California Penal Code pretty well, so you can tell my officers what charges they can expect. We'll remove your weapons from you since you know the drill. No quick moves!"

"You OK?" Jeannie asked Ismail. "All except my nose. I think those assholes broke it." "Ah, and it was such a nice looking nose," Jeannie said while smiling. She called on her cellphone requesting that her forensic team come in and collect the evidence on the chief's desk, including the Rolex and promissory note. When they arrived, Ismail removed his bloody shirt and they removed the microphone taped to the small of his back, along with the cord from the device taped to his chest. "God, I wasn't really expecting all the rough housing! Thank God they didn't find the tape," he said.

Jeannie said, "Burk and Darcy are in the van across the street. They said the taping was excellent. I'm glad that Darcy did a good job of writing you up on the Internet. It would have blown your cover if when they ran a search on you, they'd found out you're a highly decorated FBI agent." "Yeah, and good looking too," Ismail added. They both laughed as they left the police station and headed back to San Francisco.

Jeannie met with SAC Lomax and filled him in about the corruption investigation in Southern California. "Suzi rolled over like a puppy wanting its belly rubbed. She's been dating Officer Gene Foxworth for about 6 months after he caught her smoking a joint by their high school. Instead of busting her, he opted for an offered blowjob, and from there a romance developed. The chief found out about their romance, and instead of arresting his officer for sex with a minor, he discussed the criminal enterprise of blackmailing marks that entered their cozy little town using Suzi as bait. Looks like they pulled the scam at least three other times before they hit the last victim, a retired district judge who contacted the attorney general, who in turn, brought us in. That little town is going to have to find a new chief and police force really soon."

"How is Ismail doing?" he asked. "I heard that they played a little rough house with him."

"He's fine," Jeannie answered, "You know Ismail--though as nails and every girl's dream. I gave him today off since he had all the paperwork done early this morning; and if it's alright with you, I think I'll head home and get some sleep. Damn I hate getting old!"

CHAPTER 5

Jeannie reached over and shut off her alarm clock. It was 6 a.m. and she had another restless night thinking about Ricky Pinheiro, her fiancé. He had been the love of her life and now he was gone--shot to death in a blazing gun battle by a member of the Sons and Daughters of Liberty.

A homegrown terrorist group was responsible for killing the remaining magistrates of the secretive court called the Star Chamber. Joey had hired, organized, and trained the assassins who carried out the clandestine court's verdicts. A brilliant former decorated soldier of both the Iraq and Afghanistan wars, he also masterminded the successful kidnapping of a wealthy businessman's teenage daughter in the style used by the 1970's Symbionese Liberation Army. Like Patty Hearst, they were brainwashing her into believing their ideology.

Receiving a tip from a teenage Concord, California boy who had seen an update of the group on television, the terrorists' rundown safehouse was set on fire and surrounded by police including Jeannie and Pinheiro. One of the fleeing female suspects fired two random shots that ricocheted from a parked vehicle and hit Ricky. The female was killed along with three of her comrades who retreated into the crawlspace under the residence while continuing to exchange rounds with the Concord Police and Contra Costa Sheriff's Department. They were either shot or burned to death. It was later determined that their ringleader, Joey, was not among them and on the run with his kidnapped victim.

Jeannie could not clearly recall Ricky's funeral. Sure, his relatives and friends were there, including colleagues from various federal security agencies as well as her friend and partner, Ismail Flores. The priest and various high-level dignitaries said a few words, but their condolences fell on deaf ears. Ricky was gone and nothing could bring him back.

Jeannie Loomis is the Assistant Special Agent in Charge of the FBI's San Francisco bureau. In her mid-forties, the twice divorced and childless, Jeannie met Ricky Pinheiro, an agent with the Department of Homeland Security, while working a joint investigation involving three teams of jihadists intent on committing three separate fatwas for the dead al Qaeda leader, Osama in Laden. In one of their attacks, they successfully killed hundreds of individuals outside a Russian Orthodox church in the city. Their second attack was to take place at a Presidential fundraiser at the Cow Palace in Daly City at the southern border of San Francisco proper. Fortunately, all three terrorists were killed before they could execute their plans. The final target was decoded by Jeannie and her team. Learning that the target was the underwater BART system tube, Jeannie and Pinheiro enlisted the Navy SEALs to take out the terrorists before they could execute a plan that would have killed thousands.

Following several trips from Washington D.C. to further their relationship, Ricky proposed to Jeannie at a 5-star restaurant by placing an engagement ring in Jeannie's glass of wine while she visited the restroom. Without hesitation, she accepted his proposal. Unfortunately, they did not have time to plan a future together, no wedding date had been set. They had not even decided how to handle their long-distance relationship with him on the east coast and her on the west. They didn't care. Both of them were deeply in love and knew nothing could keep them apart. Jeannie had finally found her soulmate.

Ricky held off death in an unconscious state for three days with Jeannie at his side before he succumbed to his wounds. She clearly remembered Ricky being hit, but the events that took place after his shooting were foggy until the doctor informed her they lost him on the operating table following another surgery. *It's amazing how the mind seems to protect the body by pushing painful events to the back of one's mind*, she thought.

Noticing her pillowcase was wet from tears, she threw the bedding over to her right and rolled over to what had been Ricky's side of the bed. It was two months since his death, and although she could no longer pick up his scent after several washes, she still felt happy on his side. Finally, she decided it was time to get up and went to the bathroom. "OK, girl. It's time to get on with life; that's what Ricky would have wanted," she said out loud while looking at herself in the mirror. She had been offered extra time to heal from the pain of her loss by SAC (Special Agent in Charge) Lomax, but she refused. Her dad taught her that the best thing to do after a loss was to get back into a routine, and time would take care of the rest. She attended several sessions with the bureau's shrink per protocol, but did not feel she was getting anything out of the therapy sessions. Having been trained in hostage negotiations and possessing a doctorate in psychology, she knew all of the techniques he tried to use on her—all to no avail. No, instead she felt she would get what she needed by going to her cabin in the hills overlooking Lake Coeur d'Alene in Idaho. Having been there a few days, she now felt ready to return to San Francisco, the Bureau, and the home she briefly shared with Rickey.

Her first night back home in Newark, her eyes teared instantly when she saw the paint cans and supplies still on the floor where Ricky had last used them. His coffee cup was still in the sink next to hers, and the refrigerator still had leftovers from meals he had cooked-- now part of a penicillin experiment she quickly fed to the garbage disposal. It seemed as if his spirit was everywhere in the house. She showered, did her makeup, and tried to focus on other things, but her thoughts continued to return. Fortunately, her cell phone rang and she saw that it was Ismail Flores, her go-to agent and friend. He was Ricky's closest cousin. "Hello Ace. How are you?" she asked.

"Hey, that's what I am supposed to ask," he replied.

"I'm hanging in there. I'm getting ready for work and will head out the door in about 40 minutes," she said.

"Are you sure?" Ismail asked. "You know, Lomax has offered as much time off as you need."

"I know, I know; but I think I'll feel better when I'm back in the saddle. Besides, you're probably doing such a good job in my stead, I might lose my job."

"Yeah, that's probably right," he said laughing. "OK, I'll see you when you get here, boss." With that, Ismail hung up.

Jeannie got into her bright red Corvette and hit the garage door opener. She hoped to get out of the garage before her nosy neighbor, Delores, caught her. She quickly backed up and looked at Delores' house. Not seeing her, she thought the coast was clear, but before she could put the car in first gear, she heard a knock on the driver's side window. Jeannie rolled down the window. "Hi, Delores. How are you? You scared me." *Damn*, she thought. *Nosey and sneaky*! Delores picked up her poodle and said, "That's what I want to know. How are you doing honey? You're not going to work already, are you? It's only been a few months. My husband, Walter, and I think you should consider another line of work. What you do is so dangerous--like I have to tell you that. Oh, I'm sorry. I hope I didn't bring back bad memories."

Jeannie took a deep breath and tried to answer her questions. "No, I'm doing fine. Yes, I'm ready to return to work. I love my job, and this is what I feel Ricky would want me to do. No, you haven't brought up bad memories. All my memories of Ricky will always be in my heart." Jeannie noticed that Delores was forming tears in her eyes. "I'm sorry Delores, I hope I didn't make you sad?" Jeannie said.

"No, no. I'm OK. If you think this is the best thing to do, then by all means, do it," Delores said, wiping her eyes on her blouse sleeve while holding her dog in her other arm. "Remember, if you need anything, like taking out the garbage can when you're gone, just let us know."

"I will Delores. I really need to get going. You never know how the traffic's going to be on the bridge. I'll talk to you later."

"OK, and please be careful," Delores said as she put her dog on the sidewalk and started home. Jeannie got a big smile on her face wondering if Ricky in heaven was laughing about her Delores encounter.

CHAPTER 6

Jeannie knew what to expect when she entered the San Francisco FBI headquarters. Everyone expressed condolences as she walked down the hallway to her office. She had a few moments of teary eyes which she indiscreetly dabbed away. Ismail came around the corner from the breakroom carrying two cups of coffee, saving her before she lost control.

"Hey, I know you. Aren't you that famous FBI agent who stopped those terrorists from blowing up the BART tube?"

"I am, and aren't you that Portuguese Chippendale dancer who women can't keep their hands off of while secretly an FBI agent?" Jeannie asked. "Hey, don't blow my cover," he said, handing her a cup of coffee. They reached her office and upon entering she found a box of Shari's Berries on her desk with a note of sympathy from Lomax. As Ismail took a chair opposite Jeannie, she picked up her desk phone and called the SAC. "As

Arnold Schwarzenegger said, I'm back (pause). Yes sir, I want to be back (pause). No, I think I need to be doing what I love. Thank you, and thanks for the box of berries; I love them (pause). OK, I'll stop by once Ismail brings me up to speed."

Ismail did not use Jeannie's office during her absence, and her desk still held paperwork regarding their investigation of Joey and the Sons and Daughters of Liberty--the SDL. "Any new information on Joey?" she asked.

"No, that asshole's gone underground. All the bodies have been positively identified and Burk and Darcy did a remarkable job of tying everything together; but his whereabouts, shit, who knows. Lomax has put in the paperwork to get him listed on the Ten Most Wanted, but this guy is slick and smart."

"OK, so what are we working on?" Jeannie asked, grabbing a fresh yellow notepad.

"Our priority case is a recent armored van robbery. The perps got away with a cool--get this--$25 million."

"No shit?" Jeannie said. "How'd it go down?

"You know that Indian casino out there by the canyon?"

"Sure, I've been there twice after it was built. I took my mom there after we lost my dad. Their dinner buffet was outstanding, and the scenic drive was great," Jeannie said.

"Well, the casino was sponsoring a five-day $25-million-dollar World Series of Poker tournament-

-the cash ordered from the Federal Reserve before the event. The security team in the van drove the main highway to the casino, the one that goes through that 5-mile canyon stretch," Ismail started to explain. "I think I know where this is going," Jeannie said.

"We believe the suspects used the canyon to block cell phone and radio signals, then staged an accident after the armored van left the highway and entered the canyon. And get this, they jackknifed a tractor-trailer across the road. It not only completely blocked the road so the armored van couldn't turn around, it also kept out potential witnesses.

"I suppose the tractor-trailer was stolen," Jeannie said. "Correctamundo," Ismail replied. "Give the lady a prize," he added. Jeannie just smiled. *God, it feels good being back on the job*, Jeannie thought.

"They had another vehicle--a box-type truck following the armored van which was also stolen. We later found it abandoned in the casino parking lot. One of the suspects posed as a highway construction flagman and was stopping traffic coming from the opposite direction. Just after the armored van entered the canyon near a cliff, they activated an EMP device that disabled the GPS signal coming from the vehicle. The stolen tractor-trailer blocked the road which is so narrow that the armored van couldn't get around. The suspects then charged it and breached the armored doors with jaws of life, releasing knock-out gas in both the cab and the back of the van. With the guards disabled, they moved all the money to the trailing box truck, dragged the van driver from the cab and threw him into the vault area with the other two guards-- then pushed the armored van over the cliff. The impact killed all three guards.

Witnesses said that when the suspects left in the box truck, an older rust-colored van picked up the fake flagman and his equipment. As I said, the stolen box truck was left at the casino and wiped clean of any prints. DNA will probably come up negative also. Casino parking lot cameras showed two suspects get out of the box truck and jump into the rusted van; both a driver and passenger can be seen in the video. They then drove to an abandoned farmhouse where they put the loot into a Class A motorhome and vanished."

"How do you know they transferred it to a motorhome?" Jeannie asked.

"Well, the owner of the farmhouse showed up a few days later and found the rust colored van, and it matched the vehicle seen in the casino photos. Forensics found tire tracks which matched those used on a Class A. Unfortunately, that's as far as we've gotten to date."

"OK. So we know there were at least four suspects. How about their race?" Jeannie asked. "Looks like two whites, one Latino, and the fourth appears to be a native Indian," he replied.

"An Indian? Indian casino? I'm sure you're looking at a possible inside job," Jeannie said.

"All over it, but the casino is very tight-lipped about their employees, and it's not as easy as checking for a dirty bank teller."

"OK. Let me handle my phone messages so I can get caught up, then we can get the team together and do some brain-storming. By the way, thanks for covering for me," Jeannie said. "Hey, what are friends for?" Ismail remarked as he left her office.

Jeannie was three-quarters through her in-basket when Lomax called and asked her to meet him in the break room. When she arrived, he was already seated with a can of Diet Coke in his hand. "I'm sure you're getting tired of everyone asking how you are, so I won't," he said. "I'm leaving it up to your judgement whether you need more time off to heal."

"No, really. I'm fine. It's nice to be back among friends and colleagues. But you're right. Every time someone offers me condolences I break down and cry; but Tim--you know, our resident psychologist who cleared me for duty--said that crying is something the body uses to heal itself, so I'm healing myself," she said, fighting back tears.

"I'm sure with your doctorate in psychology and experience in behavioral analysis you knew every technique Tim tried to use on you. Again, if you later decide you need more time off, just let me know. OK, has Ismail got you up to speed?" he asked.

"Yes, the team's focused on the armored van theft. We have a few leads and we're all over it. Hopefully something will break soon," Jeannie said.

"That's good, because I need you to join up with the Marin County Sheriff's Department task force to help hunt for Daniel Koufax, the serial killer. It looks like he did another one last night in their backyard," Lomax responded.

"Jesus, we were so tied up with the SDL and the Star Chamber bombing, plus the Charlotte Sadler kidnapping, I wasn't following the latest on the hunt for him. How many kills is this?" she asked.

"It'll be number seven. Do you know Marin County Sheriff's Captain, Jerry Gilman?" Lomax asked.

"Not really. I know what he looks like when I see him on TV, but I don't think I've ever talked with him," Jeannie replied.

"Jerry and I go way back. He's a nice guy, but admitted to me that being placed in charge of the task force is driving him to an early grave. He specifically requested your help several weeks ago; but well, you know…" There was an uneasy silence in the breakroom, broken when Lomax handed Jeannie a note with Jerry's cell number.

"Be prepared. Jerry's going to ask you to take over the task force reins. Let Ismail handle the armored car theft and continue handling your job for now. He really did an excellent job covering for you--and give Jerry everything you can. This might be exactly what the psychologist ordered," he said as he got up, patted Jeannie on the shoulder and began to leave.

Serial killer task force! Damn, talk about jumping from the frying pan into the fire, Jeannie thought as she got up and began searching for Ismail.

Joey met Amir in the latter's detached garage in Alameda—a space used as his residence to escape San Francisco Bay Area's astronomical rent costs. Following a short greeting, Amir congratulated Joey on exploding the warehouse being used by the former secret court, the Star Chamber. Amir had provided Joey and the SDL with the three bombs they hid in flowers that were used to decorate the tables used by the clandestine judges. Following the welcoming of judges who began the tribunal, Joey was able to detonate all three bombs simultaneously with one phone call, killing and burning all judges beyond recognition. DNA and dental charts were needed for their identification.

Joey thanked Amir for congratulating him, and then asked if he had been able to secure the materials he requested several weeks earlier. Amir did not respond, instead he stood up and walked to a small portable refrigerator and opened it. He pulled out a large plastic container wrapped in bubble wrap, unwrapped it enough to show several smaller vials having a light green liquid inside each, carefully re-wrapped it, and placed it in an Igloo cooler containing dry ice. Then, grabbing a cardboard box filled with something covered by a blanket, he maneuvered both the Igloo and the box toward Joey and sat back down.

"This is what you wished," Amir said. "I must again tell you, my brother--this virus is one of the deadliest viruses on earth. It took a lot of money and convincing to persuade my connection to steal this sample from its level-four lockup."

"Has it now been engineered so it can be administered as an airborne agent?" Joey asked.

Amir pulled back the blanket covering the box and lifted up several gadgets that looked like pluggers. "Yes, it is now capable of becoming airborne and appears to be even more deadly than when it is naturally spread by green monkeys infected by bats in Uganda. In its natural state it has an 88% fatality rate. Airborne, I can only speculate how much deadlier it has become."

Amir showed Joey how the material should be transferred from the vial into the plunger devices. Satisfied that he knew how to place the deadly virus in the aerosol plungers, Joey reached into his pocket for what Amir thought was the remainder of his payment. Before Amir could react, Joey pulled out a suppressed .22 caliber revolver and shot him twice in the chest. Amir fell forward in his chair making no sounds, as Joey walked behind and shot him in the right ear. "Sorry my friend, but I cannot have any loose ends," Joey said to the corpse as he picked up his deadly cargo and left the garage.

"Hello, Captain Gillman, this is Agent Jeannie Loomis." "Oh yes, thank you for calling, Agent Loomis," Gillman replied. "Please, just call me Jeannie. SAC Lomax asked me to call you. I heard you might have another one," Jeannie said. "Unfortunately, yes," he said. "I 'm wondering if you might be able to drive over to my office so we can discuss the case and the task force. Or, if you're tied up on something, I could drive to the city and meet with you there."

"No, I can be over there right after lunch if that's convenient." Jeannie said.

"That would be great. Frankly, I'm at wits end and need all the help I can get. Is one o'clock OK?"

"Sure, I'll see you then," Jeannie replied as they hung up.

Jeannie check-in with Lomax and then left a note on Flores' desk since she had been unable to find him earlier, saying that she would be driving over to the Marin County Sheriff's Department after lunch to meet with Captain Gillman, and she would call when she got there. She would tell him that Lomax had requested he continue acting in her stead by phone instead of including it in the note.

She stopped at a Subway and grabbed a 6" hot-roast-beef on sourdough and washed it down with a diet Dr. Pepper. She had brought her laptop to the restaurant, and using their WIFI , she began searching for everything related to Daniel Koufax and the many murders attributed to him. She knew there was much more information about the cases that had not been shared with the media, but she wanted to at least have some background knowledge of the investigation before she met with Captain Gillman.

In addition to the recent murder last night, which the press was having a field day with, Koufax had been linked to six homicides--all involving white female victims. The first posting was of a white female found strangled in a Reno, Nevada motel room. The article said the police had no comment regarding evidence found at the scene. A motel maid found a "do-not-disturb" handwritten note over the doorknob, so she skipped cleaning the room that day; but when she returned the next day, the note was still there. She knocked on the door but received no answer. Using her pass-key, she slowly opened the door and announced "housekeeping" to alert anyone inside. Entering the room, she continued to the bathroom to assess how much work awaited her. There she found a nude female in the bathtub. She screamed, backed out of the room, and ran to the manager's office.

The ensuing newspaper article was of a homicide in Marin county--their first involving Koufax, although it was a "who-done-it" at the time. It was the same scenario: a nude white female found strangled in a motel room. The editors of this article somehow secured a photograph of the victim which Jeannie studied before switching back to a posting showing an earlier victim. The victims looked very similar. From her days in the behavioral analysis unit, Jeannie knew Koufax's victim-type.

Jeannie continued the Internet search while finishing off her sandwich, believing that she was now up to speed on the investigation, at least from the media's perspective, and ready to meet with Captain Gillman. Koufax was linked to six homicides: five in the Northern California region and one in Nevada. Jeannie was sure last night's kill was the sixth in California, bringing the total to seven. She already had several questions about concerns that were bugging her. Koufax, with the exception of wiping down the bathtub walls during the Nevada kill, no longer seemed interested in covering his tracks . Law enforcement now had a treasure trove of evidence including Koufax's semen specimen, his fingerprints, DNA from victims' fingernails, and signatures on motel rental agreement forms. Shit, the only thing missing was for him to leave a video recording showing him committing the crimes. Yet, he was still on the loose--always one step ahead of the police. In one case the body of the victim was still warm. It was as if Koufax was playing a game with the police--a "time game." *Catch me if you can!*

Just before reaching the Marin County Sheriff's Department, Jeannie called Ismail. "Hey boss, where are you?" "I thought we were going to brainstorm after lunch," he replied. "I left you a note. I'm over at the Marin County's Sheriff's Department. The SAC asked me to contact Captain Gillman who specifically requested that I help with the Koufax serial killer case. I'm almost there. I wanted to give you a heads-up though; Lomax said Gillman will probably be asking me to take over the task force since it's destroying his health. I don't know if you're aware, but the asshole killed another one last night."

Ismail said he was, and wished Jeannie luck since Koufax was an elusive son-of-a- bitch. "Yeah, I heard it on the news. Number seven, huh?" Ismail asked.

"Looks like it. So, you'll have to once again take over my position as Assistant SAC while working the armored van heist. Sorry to dump it on you. By the way, Lomax complimented your covering for me, so I wanted to pass that on."

"Hey, that's OK. Does your Corvette come with the job?" he asked trying to suppress a laugh. "No, sorry. But feel free to use my office and desk," she responded. "Gee, thanks," Ismail said. "Call me later this evening and let me know how the task force is progressing." Jeannie said she would.

CHAPTER 7

The Four Aces Club is located in the old downtown area of Calistoga, a small city of around 5,000 people in California's Napa Valley about 1.5 hours north of San Francisco and part of California Wine Country. There are numerous wineries within a short drive that allow visitors to see wine country as it was before freeways and fast food. There is only one two-lane road leading in and out of town, and fast-food franchises are banned by law. It is known for its hot springs and mud baths in addition to its wineries; its economy is highly dependent on tourist dollars. Former 49ers quarterback and Hall of Famer Joe Montana used to have a home and vineyard in Calistoga.

The Four Aces is a bar next to one of the oldest businesses in town--an old-style bakery. Most tourists do not venture into old town at night because they are usually tired after seeing all the daytime tourist attractions. The Four Aces cliental is made up of locals who come in to share stories of dumb tourists who are willing to pay good money to lay in hot mud or hot mineral water, or be pampered by technicians who place fish eggs on their face for $300 a pop.

Sally Yates was one of those locals. At forty-seven with raven hair worn down past her shoulders and dark brown eyes, she could really turn heads. When her parents died, she inherited a large vineyard located just out of town that specialized in growing Cabernet Sauvignon grapes, acknowledged as the king of red grapes in Napa Valley. However, Sally could not have cared less about cultivating grapes. Her foreman ran the acreage, taking care of the growth, maintenance, and harvesting of crops. As a member of several local country clubs, she was too occupied playing tennis and flirting with the men, both single and married. Divorced four times, she was always on the lookout for number five, especially if he had money or good looks. She had no desire for children, thinking it would screw up her figure. No, for Sally, a good sexual encounter three-to-four times week kept her satisfied. She had not yet found a particularly attractive female for a lesbian affair, but that door was not closed.

Sally quickly checked out the action upon entering the Four Aces. *Looks just like the normal crowd,* she thought, disappointed. She then noticed a large man sitting near the end of the bar who drew her interest. He had long blond hair--longer than hers--and very well built, looking like an NFL linebacker. Never accused of being shy, she moseyed up to him, noticing that he saw her approach. With the top three buttons of her blouse unfastened, she saw him checkout her cleavage and black lace bra. *Yeh, he's hooked*, she thought as she took a seat next to him. "Hi, I'm Sally."

"Nice car. Is that standard issue over there at the FBI?" asked Frank Gilbert, a veteran homicide investigator with the Marin County Sheriff's Department who saw Jeannie exit her red Corvette in the security parking lot. Jeannie looked in his direction and instantly recognized him.

"Frank! My God, how many years has it been?" Frank walked up to Jeannie and they embraced. "Too many. I'm so sorry for your loss." Frank said. "I worked a case with Pinheiro a few years back; the guy was a true professional. I heard you're coming over to help us with the Koufax investigation. Let me be the first to welcome you aboard."

"Thanks Frank. Please tell me you're part of the task force."

"Since the beginning, and I have to tell you, it hasn't been a who-done-it. This bastard is the luckiest fucker I've ever seen. Twice now we were only hours behind him, but he always gets away. He leaves tons of evidence--like he just doesn't care."

"You know that old saying in law enforcement: we only catch the dumb ones--and to answer your question," Jeannie said with a smile, "No, the Vette is mine and my SAC told me to start driving my assigned bureau car before other agents start putting in requests for one of their own."

"I hear that," Frank responded while laughing. "You know, you and your team did an outstanding job tracking down those terrorists. Jesus, do you know what kind of panic someone blowing up the BART tube would have caused, not only among the people here in the bay area, but across the U. S.? No one would want to take public transit again."

"Thanks, Frank. I'm fortunate to have a fantastic team working for me. So, fill me in about the task force before I meet with Captain Gillman."

"I don't want you to be broadsided, so I'll tell you confidentially that Jerry's going to ask you to take over the reins. He's in bad health, and I'm sure he'll give you the particulars," Frank said, as they entered the building.

"Jeannie, how are you?" Captain Gillman asked as he stood when Jeannie and Detective Gilbert entered his office. "Fine, and you?" Jeannie replied. "Doesn't do any good to complain. Please take a seat. Frank, maybe you could get Agent Loomis a cup of our finest?"

"You don't have to Frank. I can get some later," she said.

"It would be my pleasure. What do you take in it?" Frank asked.

"You sure? Cream and two Stevia or Sweet-and-Lows would be great," Jeannie replied. Frank said he would return shortly, so she turned her attention back to Gillman.

"Jeannie, I'm so glad you were able to break away from the bureau and help us out, but actually it's more than that." Anticipating Gilbert's return, Gillman quickly got to the point. "Jeannie, I have a bad heart condition. My doctor wants me to retire right now, but I want to put in one more year to sweeten up my retirement benefits so the wifey and I can retire comfortably."

"Gee, Jerry, I'm sorry. Are you sure it's worth your life to put in one additional year?" Jeannie asked.

"The doctor told me that if I could manage my stress level better, eat a healthier diet, and start a routine exercise regimen I should be OK, and that brings me back to why I invited you here." Detective Gilbert knocked on the door frame, announcing his return while holding a cup of coffee. "Here you go. Nothing but the finest for the FBI," he said, while handing the cup to Jeannie. "Frank," said the Captain, "Come in and shut the door."

After Frank took a seat, Gillman looked at Jeannie and said that Frank is the only other person in the department that knows the seriousness of his condition. "Jeannie, after we learned that the Reno P.D. positively identified Koufax as the killer, we realized we could turn the case over to the feds for unlawful flight to avoid prosecution. But frankly, the taskforce has done a lot of work trying to catch this son-of-a-bitch, and that we really don't want a Washington-type to come out here and screw up our chemistry. No offense to the FBI," he said.

"None taken. I completely understand your concern," Jeannie said. "Perhaps federal resources will help us catch him. His killings are now seven days apart, so his next one should be in six days."

Jeannie noticed a quick glance between Gillman and Gilbert and surmised that the real reason she was asked to come to the Marin County Sheriff's Department was about to be revealed. "Jeannie, I would like you to take over leadership of the taskforce. Lomax and I have already discussed it and he can put in the paperwork to make it official, but we didn't want to blindside you, especially after everything you've gone through."

Acting a little surprised for the sake of Detective Gilbert, Jeannie replied. "I appreciate that, but I must admit that Lomax kind of gave me a heads up about what you needed; so yes, I'll take over the reins. I just hope Frank can get me up to speed before I meet the team," Jeannie said.

"I'm sure I can do that," replied Frank with a smile on his face. "We're scheduled to meet in an hour, so how about another cup of coffee and I can fill you in," said Frank.

"Sounds good," Jeannie replied.

"Jerry, get some rest if you can. I'm sure Frank and I can handle the Koufax case pressure from here on," Jeannie said as she rose and walked out of Gillman's office with Frank.

"God Jeannie. I'm starting to feel better already," said Captain Gillman.

At 9 a.m. Lupe began working her way down the Calistoga Motel's second floor hallway, making sure that occupants who were to have checked out had left so she could clean their rooms for the next guests. She was extremely tired; she had been studying for her upcoming citizenship review and wanted to make sure she knew answers to questions she might be asked. Having five children at home, the youngest only 18-months, made it difficult, but she and her husband needed the extra money. His job as a landscaping assistant could not cut it for the family, so she became a maid for the hotel chain.

She knocked on room 21- C and announced that housekeeping was about to enter the room. There was no reply, so she felt it was OK to enter. The king size bed had obviously been used, so she quickly removed the sheets and threw them into her hopper. Finding the wastepaper baskets near the nightstands empty, so she moved to the bathroom. She immediately saw a woman's leg hanging over the side of the bathtub, blood pooled below her right arm which, like her right leg, was hanging over the side. The woman's chest had several stab wounds, and the body had an ivory appearance like a mannequin. In shock, she quickly turned and ran to the manager's office.

Within minutes of the 9-1-1 call, two officers from the Calistoga Police Department arrived at the motel and found the maid's cart in the hallway outside the door. The officers told the manager to stay outside while they entered. Officer Tim Cardoza, the senior of the two, entered the room followed by Officer John Stewart. The king size bed was void of sheets and they saw them in the maid's cart near the foot of the bed. Entering the bathroom they saw a nude female laying in the tub face up with her right leg and right arm hanging over an edge of the tub as described by the maid. The body had no pulse and was cold to the touch, and the upper torso had several stab wounds. Her right arm had been sliced horizontally as if she had committed suicide. Officer Cardoza requested that his supervisor respond to the scene.

Lieutenant Glenn Parks was a thirty-year veteran of law enforcement. Most of that duty was with the Napa County Sheriff's Department before transferring to Calistoga after the city incorporated and formed their own force. Lt. Parks never tested for a position in the investigation division; he loved the streets where the action was. Slightly overweight but in good shape for his age, he loved breaking up bar fights and driving through the canyons surrounding city Code Three while smoking a cigar.

Fuck the rules about no smoking in patrol cars. Everyone on the force had nothing but respect and admiration for the Lieutenant. He had been through hell, losing his six-year-old son from a concussion after a fall, followed by his wife dying an agonizing death from cancer a few years later. He could pull the pin anytime he desired and retire; but why, law enforcement was all he had left in his life. He knew that eventually his body would let him down and he would have to leave--not for his own safety, but the safety of his fellow officers.

Upon arrival at the motel, he entered the room, but only looked at the corpse from outside the bathroom since he did not want to contaminate the scene. Seeing the victim's face, he immediately identified her as a local--Sally Yates. He saw the stab wounds to her chest and noticed that her throat had also been cut. Thinking to himself that this looked like an overkill, he closed the door and requested that the coroner respond as well as a detective unit. He told the two officers to secure the scene and went to the manager's office, finding the maid sitting in a chair holding a cup of coffee.

Parks set down next to the maid and began asking her about the discovery. Upon concluding his interview, he asked the manager for the rental card that would have the names of room 21- C's occupants. He removed a pair of gloves from his pocket and took the card. Just as he thought: there was Daniel Koufax's signature.

A viewing of the security tapes allowed him to positively identify Koufax as the person who entered room 21- C with Sally Yates at approximately 1:13 a.m. Koufax left the room at 5:10 a.m. carrying a duffle bag, not appearing to be in a hurry or scared. He walked to a vehicle in the parking lot not covered by cameras. Parks realized that if Koufax stayed true to his M.O. (Modus Operandi) he probably took Yate's vehicle. He contacted dispatch and had them run a DMV check on any and all vehicles owned by Yates. She only had one registered to her name--a silver Maserati. He asked dispatch to issue an APB on the vehicle--no reason to wait for the detectives to respond to the scene since they would have done the same thing. Maybe this time the police would win the Time Game.

CHAPTER 8

The Marin County Sheriff's Department briefing room was packed with over nineteen law enforcement officers, in both plain clothes and uniform. All genders and races seemed to be represented, although Jeannie could care less about such things; she just wanted results. She and Frank took seats near the podium where Captain Gillman stood. Dressed in his freshly pressed uniform, he tapped the microphone and the room became silent.

"Let's get started, he said. We have just been notified that the Calistoga Police Department found another one of Koufax's victims this morning. He's keeping with his M.O. by not covering his tracks. I brought you together today to announce a change in our task force. As you know, one of Koufax's homicides took place in Reno, Nevada, making this a federal case. I had to pull some strings but was able to convince SAC Lomax of the San Francisco FBI bureau to assign

Assistant Special Agent in Charge Jeannie Loomis to take over the task force, so now we have the full force of the bureau with us. Agent Loomis will now fill you in about the particulars of the Calistoga murder and her vision for the task force--Agent Loomis," he said, motioning for Jeannie to approach the podium.

"Good afternoon," Jeannie said, as she reached the podium and looked out at the audience. She was wearing a conservative dark blue pantsuit and had placed her blond hair in a ponytail. She knew that some of those present resented the FBI intruding on their case. "First, I look forward to working with you. I recognize several of you and hope to get to know all of you as we attempt to takedown Koufax. Let me say that this is your case; the FBI is not stepping in and taking over the hard work you've done. I know the rap our agency has, deservedly or not, of taking over a case after the locals have done all the work and then taking all the credit. That's not going to happen in this case, I promise you.

As Captain Gillman said, Koufax struck again late last night or early this morning. Their investigators learned that he met the victim in a local tavern and later checked into a motel, signing the registration form using his own name. He paid cash for the room. His prints are all over the card and in the room. We have DNA that is being processed as well as items found in the motel room and on the victim. The method of death was multiple stabbings, including the victim's throat being cut followed by strangulation. Koufax was captured on security cameras as he entered the room with the victim at 1:13 a.m. and left at 5:10 a.m. The victim's car is missing and a BOLO (be on the lookout) is in effect.

Once again, he was only a few minutes ahead of us. I call it playing a "time game." I've requested a few of my agents from the San Francisco bureau office to assist each of you." Jeannie heard a few anticipated grumbles. "I stress, they are here to assist you. Even though I have taken over the responsibility of the task force, each of you has put so much time and effort into this case that you know it better than we do. Time is of the essence and I don't want to lose time. It appears that Koufax is operating on a six or seven day kill rate. Therefore, I've asked Detective Gilbert to divide each of you into squads to which I will assign my agents.

Your job is to fill in my agents with what your part of the investigation has been to date. We'll meet here at 9 a.m. tomorrow when someone from your squad will brief all of us. After that, we'll decide together what still needs to be investigated--a little brainstorming if you will. My agents are expected soon, so if you need to take care of some loose ends, do it now so we can get started. We'll meet back here at 1500 hours. I know that's not giving you much time, so I've arranged to have food and drinks delivered, so if you don't have time for lunch you can eat here." With that, Jeannie rose and walked out of the briefing room with Gilbert and Gillman.

Joey watched from the auditorium parking lot across from a food-truck mobbed with construction workers at 10 a.m. He first met the group wearing a hardhat and placed an order for a breakfast burrito and large cup of coffee. This was the third morning he had joined the group after they walked from the interior of the auditorium. They were preparing the large concert hall for the Democratic National Convention being held in Los Angeles in two weeks. Carpenters, HVAC workers, painters, electricians, you name it--they were all busy getting the place ready. Rent-a-cops were also there and they, too, took a break when the food truck arrived each morning. Joey made sure that each of the security guards got to see him there with the rest of the workers. Eventually, Joey knew that the "suits" from all federal agencies would swarm the building before the big event. Hell, the presumed nominee already had a huge attachment of Secret Service agents protecting his ass.

One worker drew Joey's attention three days earlier--same height, weight and Fu-man chu mustache as worn by Joey; they could almost be twins. In the evening when work was completed, Joey followed him to a nearby gym where the worker changed into his workout clothing before hitting the weights. Joey had no problem picking the lock on the guy's gym locker and taking his identification card with picture. He removed the picture when he got to his motel room and placed a picture of himself in the appropriate spot. The dumbass rent-a-cops only occasionally look at anyone's identification, and since he had breakfast with them recently, Joey expected no problem accessing the arena.

One guard in particular, Sam, was always discussing sports and a game he witnessed the night before. Obese to the tune of probably 280 pounds by Joey's estimate, Sam would devour three breakfast burritos and two donuts, washing it all down with a large hot chocolate or juice. Joey made a mental note to start watching a few sporting events and using that as an excuse to interact with Sam. For two consecutive days he discussed NFL trades, NBA games, and even joked about figure skating. Tomorrow he would do a dry run, carrying in a tool belt and entering the ceiling area to select the best site for his plan. If unchallenged, he would start bringing in his materials and start their assembly. In less than two weeks, law enforcement would close the place down before the convention and start security checks. By then, he would be well out of the danger zone.

If everything went as planned, thousands of liberal left-leaning radical democrats would be inhaling the world's most deadly virus, sharing it with their fellow constituents as well as their loved ones at home. For three days, they would spread the disease showing no signs of infection until it was too late, and by then the Democratic Party would severely be decimated, taking their warped un-American ideology to hell.

Joey had a history of making things happened when society was not quick enough to rectify the socialization of America. He was the former head of the assassination squad who worked for the secret court called the Star Chamber. He liked the idea of a clandestine court, judging elites in absentia, and if found guilty having the death penalty enacted at once. Unfortunately, some smart-ass female FBI agent interfered, and the court in panic mode began killing off his assassins before going dark. After laying low for a period of time with the few remaining members of his assassination squad, Joey got even by blowing them up when court reconvened.

CHAPTER 9

Flores stood in front of six agents under his command, including IT agents Darcy and Burk. Darcy and Burk were an integral part of Jeannie's team, and involved in both the Star Chamber investigation and the recently thwarted terrorist cell attempt to blow up the BART tube. Agents Tim O'Flannery and his partners Jaime Nelson, Sam Donaldson, and Ron Lucas all sat near the front of the briefing room. "OK, Assistant SAC Loomis will be absent for an unknown period of time assisting the Marin County Sheriff's Department with the Koufax serial case. That means the armored van heist is all ours. I had Darcy and Burk put what we know so far up here on the board (pointing to a large whiteboard). As we know, most armored car jobs are done by someone on the inside, so here are pictures of the dead guards and background summaries. Initially, we need to think of the possibility that one or more of these guards were involved in the theft and later double-crossed.

The fact that one of the suspects appears to be a Native American needs to be investigated along with the casino. I've already tried to get the casino to assist, and it's been like pulling teeth without Novocain, but it still needs to be explored. This will be my responsibility. If I can convince them to give up their surveillance tapes quickly, perhaps we can run a facial recognition on the perps and get lucky," Flores said while looking at Darcy and Burke who would handle facial recognition if they got the tapes.

"Tim," continued Flores, "I want you and Jaime to focus on the driver of the armored van. Sam, you and Ron take this guard (pointing to a photo). Darcy and Burk will take him (pointing to another photo). Everything goes through me and I will determine when we all need to get together again. OK, let's hit it people."

Tim and Jaime told Sam and Ron they would do the background investigation on all the guards so the agents wouldn't trip over each other at the security firm. They first ran all three deceased guards through NCIC and found no record on any of them. The manager of the armored van service anticipated the bureau's need for personnel packages of each guard, and was extremely helpful upon Tim and Jaime's arrival.

The driver, Ralph Gerston, was 56-years old. He had been employed by the security firm for 18-years and had always received outstanding performance reviews. His hiring package showed that he had completed a polygraph examination and a glowing background check before hiring. He was twice divorced with two adult children from his first marriage and living with his third wife. Numerous random drugs checks all came back clean. The only thing Jaime and Tim learned from their interview with the manager was that Gerston was not scheduled to drive on that date. Another driver called in sick, and Gerston jumped at the opportunity to pick up some overtime.

Wallach (Wally) Flynn was fairly new to the security firm with four years prior experience working for a competitor. Twenty-nine and single, he had only received one written reprimand for twice showing up late, and never showed up late again. Like Gerston, he never failed a drug test nor was suspected of any wrong doing other than tardiness.

Ron Goldman was forty-seven years old and was the supervisory guard on-duty that day. His retired on a medical disability from the SFPD, but after several years in semi-retirement decided to supplement his retirement income by working for the armed guard service. His background, like the others, was clean. "Not a red flag among them," Tim said to Jaime, not expecting or receiving a response. "We need to check their bank records, where they lived, and see if they were living beyond their means." Jaime agreed, and they headed for Gerston's residence.

"We also need to track down and talk with all their listed relatives, friends, co-workers and people they listed as reference on their employment sheets," Jaime added.

"Yep, a lot of work ahead of us, that's for sure," Tim said.

Gerston and his family lived in a trailer court in Burlingame. It was a well-kept park with a community swimming pool and nice landscaping. His wife Gloria answered the door on the second knock. Slightly overweight with dishwater blond hair, she allowed the two agents to enter after they showed their identification. In the living room, Jaime and Tim saw numerous sympathy cards displayed on an end table.

"First, we both want to offer our condolences for your loss," said Jaime in a soft voice. "Thank you," Gloria said. "He was a good man," she added.

"We just have a few routine questions to ask you, if you feel up to it?" said Jaime. "Anything I can do to help you find the assholes who killed my husband," she replied.

Jaime and Tim took turns asking mundane questions about where they met, how long they had lived in the mobile home park, if she were employed, and the status of their marriage. They then got more specific and asked questions about their financial situation and how her husband felt about his job.

Gloria showed no objection to their line of questioning, and appeared to sincerely and truthfully provide all the information they requested. Upon concluding their questioning, Jaime asked if they might conduct a search of the mobile home, without indicating what they were looking for. Gloria invited them to do so, but first Jaime pulled a volunteer consent form from her briefcase asking her to sign. "We really appreciate you doing this for us Mrs. Gerston. Otherwise we would have to secure a search warrant and go the formal route which takes a lot of valuable time."

"Not a problem," Gloria said, "I want those bastards caught as soon as possible." Tim and Jaime began their methodical search of the mobile home, looking for any sign that Ralph Gerston had planned or participated in the robbery. They came up empty.

In their bureau car heading to the office, Jaime and Tim compared their feelings about Gerston. "I could be wrong, but I don't think Ralph had anything to do with the robbery. Poor guy was in the wrong place at the wrong time. He hoped to pick up some extra money, probably to help him pay for his two previous divorces, and it wasn't his lucky day," Tim said.

"I think your read on him is spot on. It seemed to me that Gloria was very much in love with him. They don't appear to have been living beyond their means. Sure, he could have a hidden bank account that Gloria doesn't know about, but my gut says no," Jaime replied. "Like you said, wrong place at the wrong time."

Agents Donaldson and Lucas drove across the Bay Bridge to Oakland to perform a search warrant on the apartment of Paul Carlson, one of the two guards that were in the vault section of the van. From the information that agents O'Flannery and Nelson provided, they knew he lived alone and hoped to find the apartment manager to check out his residence. "What a crappy neighborhood," Nelson said as they arrived at the apartment complex. "Guess that's all he could afford on a guard's salary," replied O'Flannery.

Not finding the complex manager initially, they located Apartment #11 on the second floor. They climbed the stairs that at one time had supported anti-slip treads, but now had been reduced to glue-backing residue. They knocked on the door and received no answer. Looking down they saw a poorly maintained swimming pool containing deep green algae. "Want to take a dip after we perform the search warrant?" Nelson asked. "After you," came the reply.

"Can I help you?" asked an older white male in his sixty's wearing a green maintenance shirt and matching jeans, looking up at the agents from the swimming pool area.

"Are you the manager?" asked O'Flannery.

"Manager, maintenance, grounds keeper. You name it," he responded.

"I'm FBI agent O'Flannery and this is my partner, Agent Nelson." Both displayed their badges.

"FBI! There's no terrorists in that apartment. It belongs to Paul Carlson, but if he didn't answer the door, he's probably at work. He's a security guard, but I don't know where he works."

"Can I get your name?" asked Nelson. "Sure, I'm Walter Simpson, but people here in the complex just call me Wally."

"Wally, Mr. Carlson was killed yesterday in an armored car robbery and we need to execute a search warrant on his premises. I am glad you're here; we really didn't want to force entry."

"I'm glad you didn't. This fucking place is so old and rundown that to replace a door is a bitch, I can tell you. Let me climb the damn stairs and I'll let you in." By the time he reached apartment #11 he was totally out of breath. "Damn cigarettes," he said as he pulled a large ring of keys from his belt. He opened the door and they were met with the smell of mildew and cat litter. Instead of allowing Walter in, Nelson told him they would let him know when they were through.

"OK, but like I told you, he's not a terrorist. If you're looking for a terrorist, there's a camel jockey in apartment #27 you might want to check out." So much for political correctness, both agents thought.

After thanking Walter who got the hint he was no longer needed, each agent took half of the apartment and started their search. A growl came from a closet in one of the two bedrooms. An overweight calico cat quickly ran out and into the bathroom where

O'Flannery secured it until they completed their search. A stack of used Playboy magazines was found on a bedroom nightstand with a few emptied beer bottles. The second room was pretty much empty except for a cheap weight-lifting bench and dumbbells. There were no pictures on any of the walls and only a few Sport Illustrated magazines were in the front room. An off-brand flat-screen television was sitting on a kitchen table that had been placed in the front room. A coffee table had replaced it in the kitchen--still littered with yesterday's meals.

Satisfied with their search and finding nothing of value, they secured the door and tracked down Wally, thanking him as they left. They told him about the cat in the apartment and asked if Wally could take care of it. "God damn cats. I guess I could. You guys going to check out #27? I know of at least one terrorist living there" he commented.

Neither Nelson or O'Flannery responded.

CHAPTER 10

The briefing room was packed wall-to-wall with local and county law enforcement officers, supplemented with federal agents from Jeannie's office. Most had helped themselves to food and drinks located in the back of the room. Preciously at 1500 hours, Jeannie approached the podium. "Good afternoon," she said. "I'll give each team a few minutes to select a spokesperson to give a synopsis of your teams' actions to date. Keep it pithy."

Ten minutes later, Jeannie took to the podium again. "Let's start with this group," Jeannie said, pointing to a team located toward the rear of the room. A female detective, probably 10 years older than Jeannie, stood and addresses the gathering. "To save time, I'll not review the particulars regarding Koufax's background. Instead, our group wants to review the suspect's kills."

She clicked a tab on her computer and a picture of Koufax appeared on the screen behind Jeannie.

"Apparently, many women find his appearance appealing. Using his appearance and personality, he trolls bars until he spots his particular type which appears to be twenty to thirty year old females with long hair and nice looking body. Using his charm, we believe he talks them into renting a room with him, except for his kill near the hospital; I'll come back to that later. Once inside the motel room, something snaps and he goes wild. He's not content with just strangling his victims; during most of his kills, he takes his time, stabbing, slicing their bodies, and in two cases, leaving bite marks." As she spoke, she continued to advance to appropriate slides showing his viciousness.

Various speakers spoke until all groups had reported. Jeannie had pretty much surmised earlier what she heard in the presentations--Koufax makes no attempt to conceal his identity; he leaves his prints and DNA at kill sites. There are numerous security camera photos of him with his victims. He signs his real name on motel rental agreement forms, and he uses his victim's cars between kills. Bottom line: he isn't trying to hide. He was known to brag that he could not get caught. The element of time was on his side--or so he thought.

"Thanks everyone. I'm very impressed with your efforts. I think it's time to ratchet up our game with Mr. Koufax. A reward will be posted tomorrow morning for information leading to his arrest. We'll start issuing multiple media blitzes and saturate television with his pictures. I'll personally take care of these actions. Patrol units will warn females on the street and bartenders about the tactics he uses to reel in his victims. I'll be assigning each team various action items, but as for the purpose of this meeting, I've wanted to share with you our strategy going forward.

We'll reach out to truckers with the latest information we have regarding the vehicle Koufax was last seen using. This will give us more eyes than just those of the CHP (California Highway Patrol). God forbid, if he strikes again, the first unit on the scene should immediately run a DMV check of the victim's vehicle and request that a BOLO to be shared with patrol units and truckers.

It appears that Koufax is due to hit again in roughly six days. That doesn't give us much time, but we need to go back and make sure all friends, relatives, and associates are re-interviewed to see if they've been contacted by him. More importantly, try to contact those individuals you weren't able to interview before. With most of his kills happening in Marin County, he must be very familiar with the area. Perhaps he grew up here. His friends and relatives need to be interviewed again. We need to go back and track them down. I've asked that your narcotics teams visit bars during the time that Koufax tends to show up and maybe, just maybe, we'll luck out and find him sitting on a barstool."

That evening, Paul Johnson, a Pacifica motel manager, called to say that someone who looked like Koufax had just checked into his motel. Local police responded and surrounded the front and back of the individual's room. Jeannie was notified and requested an update after contact was made. After checking his identity, the officers quickly eliminated him as Koufax. "Shit!" Jeannie said after dispatch advised her.

News conferences were occurring daily, and Jeannie was putting in 18-hour days, but it did not faze her. Photographs of Koufax continued to be plastered on every network television news program. More and more sightings came in--but still no Koufax. Paid cable and satellite news stations including Fox News and the One American News Network were saturated with updates about Koufax. Jeannie showed possible routes Koufax might take to get out of the state, as well as photos of his old haunting grounds and kill sites.

Jeannie contacted Lomax and requested that Koufax make it to the FBI's Ten Most Wanted list. This increased the amount of resources allocated to Jeannie and the task force, plus the media ate it up. Truckers continued to help search the highways, reporting several possibilities that did not turn out not to be Koufax.

"How the fuck could this son-of-a-bitch avoid the tight noose we've placed around him?" Jeannie asked Frank Gilbert over a lunch they shared. "He's like a ghost. No one sees him, but he walks among us. You know, his victims' age group falls in the Millennial group. I think they're also referred to as Generation Y," Frank said.

"Meaning?" Jeannie asked.

"They grew up with technology, and they rely on it to perform their jobs better. Armed with smartphones, laptops, and other gadgets, this generation is plugged in 24/7. They like to communicate through email, text messaging, and whatever new social media platform that becomes available; you know, things like Twitter, Instagram, and Tic Tock. That's all their friends and colleagues use. Shit, that's all they use! This is a generation that can't even imagine a world without the Internet or cell phones," Frank responded.

"So?" Jeannie asked.

"...nurtured and pampered by parents who didn't want to make the mistakes of the previous generation; millennials are confident, ambitious, and achievement-oriented."

"Where are you going with this, Frank?" Jeannie asked.

"What I'm getting at, is that Koufax's victims are millennials that only care about what is new in technology and their job. They don't follow the news or politics. They don't really watch television. They use journalism and entertainment to get their news, and we know how the liberals have taken over these venues. I mean, if some rap star tells them who to vote for, that's all they need. Be damned, understanding issues or biasness. This is all the guidance they use on how to vote. We need to use their sources of enlightenment to get through to them. In other words, we need to go on Twitter, Instagram, all the social media platforms. Let's recruit some of their idols and have them inform the females about Koufax. Let's put some fear into their lives."

"Frank, that's a great idea." Jeannie paused for a minute, lost in thought. "Here's what I want you to do. Contact as many officers as you can and see if they have sons, daughters, and anyone who falls into the Generation Y group. See if any of them would be excited about using their skills working with social media to catch this guy. Once you get a list, I'll try to free up two of my IT wizards in San Francisco who will work with them and put the heat on various social media giants to cooperate. Jump on that now."

CHAPTER 11

On Thursday, Sam Winston--owner of Rack-em-Up pool hall in Oakland--called a 9-1-1 operator stating that Koufax was playing pool in his establishment. His description matched Koufax to the tee. Oakland P.D. responded, but once again, it was not the suspect. Then the task force got a reliable tip. Yates' stolen car was found at a San Francisco Greyhound bus terminal; several teams were dispatched to the scene. Security video was pulled and reviewed. Koufax was seen abandoning the car, but not purchasing or boarding a bus. No vehicles had been reported missing. Did he do an auto hijack and now have a new victim? Hundreds of leads continued to pour in, but none provided any information regarding Koufax's whereabouts.

On Friday morning an Aileen Cordell called the Marin County Sheriff's Department. Whispering, she told the dispatcher that Daniel Koufax was at her house. She said he was a distant cousin and she had not seen him in a long time. She knew from the news that he was being sought for several homicides. Currently, he was opening her garage to put his car inside.

Several patrol units were quickly dispatched to Cordell's residence located on the south side of the county. Within minutes Cordell heard squelching tires and saw red and blue lights come up her driveway while patrolmen closed off the street. Officers armed with handguns and shotguns advanced to the detached garage and residence. Frightened and not sure what to do, Cordell squatted down behind her favorite recliner. The police began banging on the door, demanding that Koufax come out. Cordell finally found the courage to shout out to the officers that he was not inside, but in the garage. As this discourse was taking place, officers had already searched the garage and found it empty. Once again, for some reason, Koufax had left seconds before their arrival. He won the game again.

Jeannie had been living in a four-star motel in San Rafael. Not wanting to drive all the way across the bay to pick up fresh clothing, she opted to visit a Ross Store and add to her wardrobe. Both Frank and Captain Jerry Gillman had invited Jeannie to their respective homes for dinner, but being a workaholic, she declined the offers. After putting in 16-18 hour days, she was content picking up fast food and continuing to work in the motel room. There, she continued to study resources she had in place and brush up on items scheduled for the next day.

On one wall, similar to the practice she did at home, Jeannie plastered pictures of Koufax, his victims, kill sites, and post-it notes. *What was she missing*? she asked herself over and over. She took a cool shower and wrapped her hair in a towel, then laid on the bed and stared at the items on the wall. *If this guy is playing a time game, then he has to feel confident in beating our response time to the scene of his kills*, she said to herself. Concentrating on the kills in Marin County, and even the one in Calistoga, Jeannie knew that the response time was within a few hours. The response time was getting closer to the kill time.

"OK, asshole! Let's see how you do this. Let's see how you're winning the time game," Jeannie said to her picture gallery on the wall. "You don't feel threatened in the bars where you troll for your victims. They're from Generation Y so more than likely they're unaware that you're among them. You pick out your type and use your charm to get them to drive you to a vehicle or motel room. Then you strike. Maybe you had already killed the woman you set on fire in the truck. Is that what you did Daniel? You first killed her in a motel room and then discarded her body in her truck? If so, will we ever find that motel room?

In most kills, I know you conned them into entering a motel room, you fuck. Once inside, you take your time torturing them and conveniently place their bodies in the tub. You steal their cars when you decide to leave, and since the victim isn't going to report their car stolen, you have time to make your get-away."

Not expecting a response from the wall, she continued to address it anyway. "But even now, with the media all over you, you beat us each time. How?" Jeannie yelled, surprising herself. She smiled and thought Ricky was probably laughing at her up in heaven. That was the first time in a long while that her thoughts strayed from the investigation to Ricky. "What was the one thing consistent in all the kills"? she asked the wall. Victim type. Type of bar. Time of night. Use of his charm. *Shit,* she thought, *I'm still missing something*. While in thought, her cell phone went off. It displayed an unknown number--probably someone from the sheriff's office. She answered, and to her surprise it was her neighbor, Delores.

"Hi Jeannie. I hope I am not interrupting you and your chase to capture that awful serial killer. That's all Walter and I have been watching on television. We only watch Fox News since those other channels are so biased, or as the President calls them, fake news. Hope you catch him soon, but if that SOB tries to break into my house and have his way with me, he's going to eat lead I tell you. So how are you doing honey?"

I know you're laughing your heart out Ricky, she thought as she tried to respond to Delores. "Hi, Delores. No, you're not interrupting me at this moment. I'm about ready to get some sleep so we can continue our investigation tomorrow. By the way, thanks for taking care of my garbage while I'm so busy."

"Oh goodness. No need to thank me for that. What are neighbor for?" she replied. "You know, Walter and I thought about you last night. We were watching a movie called 'Highwaymen.' Have you seen it?" she asked. Before Jeannie could answer, Delores continued. "It has Kevin Costner and Woody Harrelson in it. I don't care much for Harrelson's politics but as an actor he's not bad." Before Jeannie had time to respond, Delores continued. "Anyway, the movie's about the chase for Bonnie and Clyde--you know--the outlaw lovers of the late 1920s and 30s. At the time, even your former boss, J. Edgar Hoover, and the technology of the FBI couldn't catch the elusive couple. Instead, it took the characters played by Costner and Harrelson to haunt the areas the couple seemed to use to escape, and finally someone came forward and they ambushed them."

"First Delores, no, I haven't seen the movie, but I'll put it on my list to watch. J. Edgar Hoover died in 1972 so he was never my boss. All agents study the Bonnie and Clyde case in the FBI academy and, and……Delores, you just gave me an idea worth checking out. I need to go. Thanks again for taking care of my house. Goodbye."

"What? What did I say that will help?…" those were the last words Jeannie remembered Delores saying as she hung up. She immediately called Frank and woke him up. “Frank, I think I know the direction we need to focus on to catch this asshole.”

CHAPTER 12

Jeannie arrived at the Marin County Sheriff's department before the graveyard shift ended their watch. Carrying a cup of Dutch Brothers coffee and a cinnamon roll, she quickly entered the empty and quiet task force meeting room . She sat at the table closest to the huge whiteboard and just stared at the material displayed there while pulling pieces of her cinnamon roll apart, dipping them in the mocha as she ate.

Frank was the next to arrive, carrying two cups of coffee. "Gee, you beat me. What did you do, sleep here last night? And I see you've already got coffee," he said.

"No, just got here, and I'm ready for my second cup. Thanks! OK, last night I got a call from my nosy neighbor who asked me if I'd ever seen the movie, 'Highwaymen.' Have you seen it?" Jeannie asked while finishing her roll and starting on the coffee Frank brought in.

“In fact, I have. It was on Netflix the other night, and me and the wife enjoyed it. Two former Texas Rangers were reluctantly called out of retirement by their governor to chase down and capture Bonnie and Clyde. You mean that movie?” Frank asked. “Don’t tell me, you want to set up an ambush by blocking a road you think they’ll take, and then when they stop we come out of the bushes with guns blazing.”

“That’s the right movie, but no. With the political climate dictated by our liberal press, I think if we did they would turn Koufax into a martyr killed in cold blood by zealous law enforcement, even questioning and counting how many rounds we used and asking why we didn’t get him to surrender.”

“Yeah, you’re probably right,” Frank said. “Different time period where the bad guy is the bad guy. What the hell has happened to society?” he asked.

“I know what you mean,” Jeannie said, “I haven’t seen the movie, but my neighbor said the two retired Texas Rangers chased the criminal lovebirds all over the southern United States and weren’t getting anywhere. They were always several steps behind--just like us.

“Yeah, that’s right. A female governor had to bow to the pressure she was getting in the newspapers and reluctantly had to unretire two Texas Rangers who couldn’t get ahead of the duo. Finally, it dawned on them that the Burrow gang seemed to revisit haunts of their past--one, because they were extremely familiar with their surroundings, and two, they received protection from friends and relatives," Frank said. "OK, but, I still don't get it. You got insight from your nosy neighbor's information? How?" Frank asked, while reaching for his coffee and staring at Jeannie.

"With the exception of the Koufax kill in Reno, all the kills took place in Marin or Napa county, right?" Not waiting for an answer, Jeannie continued. "He scouts for his victims by trolling in local bars. Using his charm, he cons them into going into a motel room, or at least be alone with him. He kills them and then steals their car. We discover the homicide, but even knowing the make and model of victim's cars, we can't find him. He has to be hiding out with friends or relatives who help him stash the cars. I haven't figured out the motivation of those helping him, but my hypothesis seems to fit the pattern he's using. It's just like the help Bonnie and Clyde received during their gangster years. What do you think?"

Initially, Frank did not respond. He took another sip of coffee and just looked at Jeannie. "You know, I think you figured this out. The reason he's winning what you call the 'Time Game' is because he's able to find safe shelter immediately after his killings. All of our efforts in alerting the CHP, the truckers, the BOLOs are worthless since he's already secluded in the confines of people he knows. Trouble is, I don't know where to go from here. Do you?"

"We need to ramp up interviews with relatives, acquaintances, friends, and co-workers, especially those we've been unable to contact. We need to turn up the heat since I feel it's one of them who's protecting Koufax; let's really lean on those we have gut feelings about. Threaten them with being an accessory and lying to a federal agent, and so on. By applying the heat, maybe someone among his friends and relatives will reconsider the protection they're providing and shut him out. This will reduce his 'safe' area. You realize, there's only a few days left before he'll strike again. He has to be feeling the itch by now."

Joey approached security guard Sam and offered him a donut from a bag he was holding in one hand while carrying a large cardboard box. Sam did not hesitate, taking the donut while adding his thoughts about a game they both watched the night before. The cardboard box contained another device that Joey would be installing that morning in the auditorium. With eight days left, he was way ahead of schedule.

As Joey worked in the ceiling area of the arena's west wing he listened to a talk show host on his iPhone, commenting to himself in either agreement or disagreement. The topic was how lawmakers around the country, but especially in cities managed by Democrats, are finding new ways to make American citizens' lives harder, but easier for armed thugs and robbers. The host brought up New York City's new bail law that puts criminals back on the street immediately after being arrested. Not surprisingly, crime has surged. He went on to discuss another new law, again in New York, to help criminal defendants. The prosecution is now required to turn over witnesses names and addresses to gang members' lawyers.

"Gee! What asshole came up with that idea? This is why New York is what it is now. Do the right thing, and you can now be killed by predators the government is protecting. That's why things are so fucked up," Joey said to himself as he tightened a bolt.

"Hey, you OK up there?" came a voice just below Joey. "Yeah, I'm OK. What's up?" Joey replied to a black electrician working just below him.

"Nothing. I just heard you yelling and cursing and wanted to make sure you were alright."

"Yeah, I was just commenting about the shit that's going on in New York. Can you believe it?" Joey asked.

"Screw New York. That place has become a cesspool if you ask me. My son-in-law came to visit the wife and me a few months ago. He came from South Africa and asked us if we had ever visited New York. I told him what I thought about that shit hole, but he decided to visit it on his return trip home. He texted us and said he was accosted by a panhandler, and when he called the police they basically told him, 'Welcome to New York' and never responded. OK, since you're all right, I'd better get back to work before the boss has my ass."

Joey continued his work, enjoying the topics discussed on the talk show. Next up was that witch, the Speaker of the House and her rebuking the President for calling MS-13 gang members "animals." She said the President was more immoral than the gang members he insulted. In other words, the President is a sinner, but the MS-13 gang members were God's children. "What the fuck!" Joey said, and then realized that maybe he was speaking too loudly. He did not want to draw attention to his work. His actions would soon wake up America and put a dagger through the heart of the radical left. But now with the devices in place for the big event, it was time to screw with his favorite FBI agent, Jeannie Loomis.

That day and the following, Joey visited various areas of the vast building, making sure he was seen by co-workers. By doing this, Joey felt that if workers were questioned later they could not say for certain where he worked. His wandering was just an element of his handywork to confuse and mess up the future investigation.

CHAPTER 13

Burk and Darcy arrived at the Salter house--the home of the other guard killed in the armored car vault. Having just turned twenty-nine with a wife seven months pregnant and expecting their first child, Salter had recently been honorably discharged from the Army where he had been a military police officer. Having applied for a position with the Hercules Police Department, he temporarily took the security job since he knew the background investigation necessary for him to become a police officer would take time.

"Hello, Mrs. Salter, I'm FBI agent Darcy Warner and this is my partner agent Burk. We are following up on the armored car robbery and the unfortunate killing of your husband. First we both want to extend our condolences.

"I'm not Debbie, I'm her sister. But, please come in," she said, opening the door. Burk and Darcy entered and found three individuals sitting on a couch in the living room. The female in the center was pregnant, dabbing her swollen eyes with a tissue. "Please agents," Debbie said, motioning toward a small couch.

Darcy again extended their condolences to Debbie Salter who thanked them. Hoping not to upset her unnecessarily, Darcy and Burk asked softball questions before gingerly focusing on the Salter's finances and marriage, finally leading to a request for a volunteer search of the residence, even though they had secured a search warrant.

As Debbie continued to sob with family members on the larger of the two sofas, Darcy and Burk began their search. Searching the master bedroom and finding nothing, they began walking down the hallway to bedroom number two. The hallway walls were hung with numerous photos, mostly of their wedding. Darcy stopped and pointed at a picture on the wall that drew Burk's attention to it. One of the photos was a group picture of the Salter's, their parents, and a male Native American. Burk removed the picture and started back to the front room, being met halfway by Debbie Salter's sister. "Can you tell me who this individual is?" Burk asked. "Sure, that's my brother-in-law's Army buddy, Johnny Loma. They served in Iraq at the same time and became close friends."

"Do you know his name and address?" Darcy asked, as Debby joined them. "Why? You don't suspect Johnny had anything to do with Jerry's death, do you?" asked Debbie.

"It's routine to track down and interview friends, neighbors, co-workers--anyone who might shed light on a suspect, that's all," said Burk.

Debbie removed her cellphone from her pocket and scanned through the contacts list. Finding what she was searching for, she stopped and gave Burk Loma's cellphone number and address. "Do you happen to know where he works?" asked Darcy. "Yes, he works security for that Indian casino near the coast."

Flores brought the team together at 0930 hours on Monday. He had asked Darcy to pick up bagels and cream cheese since it would be a working brunch. Things should move quickly now that the Indian had been identified, Flores thought. After everyone made their food selection and grabbed a coffee or tea, Flores got started.

"This is Johnny Loma. Thanks to Darcy and Burk, we now know that not only was he a friend of one of the guards killed in the robbery, but also a former employee at the casino. When I say former, I mean he left employment without notice three days before the robbery. He's ex-military, having served two tours of duty with Jerry Salter in Iraq. We don't know too much about him to date. Darcy and Burk will work on that. I'll be heading to the casino, this time with a search warrant for his employment records as well as anything else I can find.

Tim, you and Jaime start putting together packets on the other two guards so that some prick defense attorney won't accuse us of jumping the gun and simply focusing our investigation on Loma and not the other suspects. OK people, I'm starting to see light at the end of the tunnel. Let's meet back here at 4 p.m. and hopefully we'll have enough to start putting people in jail."

Just after lunch, Flores was notified that someone was on the line claiming to have seen the truck involved in the Indian Casino heist described on television . "Great," Ismail said to the receptionist giving him the update, "Another good Samaritan who wants to collect on the $100,000 reward, I bet."

Two hours later, Bob Peterson arrived at the bureau. At first glance, Flores realized he had to reassess his gut feelings about Peterson. At age 71, but still in good shape, Peterson arrived in a full suit. He told Flores that on the day of the casino robbery, he was out walking his deaf 16 year old dog. Peterson has to concentrate on watching his dog even though he's on a leash, since the dog sometimes darts into traffic and has come close to being hit a few times; he cannot hear an approaching vehicle. He only recently saw information on TV about the robbery. Fed up with all the biased news, he said he rarely turns the tube on.

That day a rust colored pickup truck drew his attention since it was traveling at a high rate of speed which, he said, is unusual in his subdivision. It made what Peterson described as a "poor Hollywood stop" at the stop sign where he was about to step off the curb with his dog. He said he got a glimpse of the passenger in the truck and remembers two letters on the California license plate—"D" and "S," but he couldn't remember the order.

Flores excused himself and called Agent Steve Murray, a forensic hypnotist. His schedule was clear, and after asking Peterson if he would submit to hypnosis session, he walked him Murray's office. Flores also arranged for Annette Warren, a forensic artist, to be present--hoping that under hypnosis Peterson could describe the passenger in more detail. *Slowly, but surely, all the pieces are coming together,* Ismail thought as he made it to the break room for a soda.

CHAPTER 14

Koufax was edgy. It had been six days since he killed Yates and the urge to kill was uncontrollable. Looking at trophies he kept of his victims did not help. He needed to see the fear in their eyes as their life left them. It was getting harder and harder to avoid recognition on the street and many of his so-called friends and acquaintances seemed unavailable when he tried to contact them. He needed to break out of his pattern and leave Marin county. Calistoga was too small, and he knew someone there would remember or recognize him from all the television exposure. *San Francisco might be a great place to hunt*, he thought to himself. *Shit, with all the crap going on in that third-world city, I should be OK. The only problem is that I don't really know the area well, and I have no friends or relatives there. I need to think this one out.*

The next evening Koufax was in downtown San Francisco. He checked in at the cheapest motel he could find near Fisherman's Wharf and began looking for a suitable bar off the beaten track. Eventually he found a bar called "Cheers." *Not a very original name*, he thought; *but whatever*. He walked in and only saw a few customers, all males. He glanced at his watch and realized it was only 4 p.m., so most of the younger crowd he enjoyed would not be off work until another hour or so.

He left the bar and found a small McDonald's squeezed between two other business, thinking the cost of rent there must be a bitch. He walked into the cramped restaurant and saw transvestites, a few fags kissing, and some chick with her hair dyed in three colors and sporting so many earrings and facial piercings she looked like an overstuffed pin cushion. *God*, he thought; *ugly with a capital U*. He placed his order, picked it up when ready, and headed outside to eat rather than remain inside.

He noticed a couple of females entering the neighboring bar who, based on their attire, appeared to have just left work. *Things are starting to look up*, he thought. He finished his Big Mac, fries and Coke, and after popping a breath mint in his mouth returned the bar. He spotted the two females sitting at the bar and sat two seats down from them, noticing he had caught the eye of one of the women. He ordered a beer and reached for some bar nuts, then looked at her for a long time. She blushed and glanced away, only to return his stare with a smile.

He summoned the bartender and requested drinks for the ladies, throwing down two ten-dollar bills, hoping that would cover the cost. The bartender picked up the bills, made, and then served the drinks to the two. One of them only gave a quick smile and returned her attention to her friend; the other one mouthed "thank you" and winked at Koufax. *Got her*, he thought.

They left the bar together, deciding to take a walk around Pier 39 and Fisherman's Wharf. She told Daniel her name was Cynthia, but that she preferred Cindy. When the walk concluded, they drifted to Koufax's cheap motel room. Once inside, Koufax quickly turned Cindy around to face him, something she interpreted as his first move toward intimacy. She was wrong. Danial placed his hands around Cindy's throat and began squeezing her last breath out of her. She tried to struggle, but he was extremely strong and she could put up little resistance. After she died, he placed her on the motel bed and stripped her nude. In a frenzy, he began biting on her breasts until he bite off part of her flesh, then reached into his rear pants pocket while dripping saliva and blood from his mouth and pulled out a folded knife. He began savagely stabbing Cindy' chest and abdomen. He grabbed her arms and inserted the knife blade on the inside of her arm to the rear of her elbow and cut a long line down to her wrist, and did the same to the other arm. Somewhere during the ritual, he felt himself climax in his shorts. Removing his clothes, Koufax showered and redressed, finally carrying the lifeless body to the shower and positioning it against the wall supporting the faucets and shower head. He did not turn on the water.

Maria Ruiz hated her job, but as an illegal alien, earning $12 on hour changing sheets in a motel was all she could get. Her husband poured concrete, also making a meager salary of $15 an hour. With four kids and rent that always seemed to go up, they lived paycheck to paycheck. The only bright side to her job was that the cheap motel was near the wharf and she loved the smell of the bay in the morning when she arrived for work. When she completed her job in the early evening, the salty air helped clear her sinuses irritated by the smoky rooms she cleaned.

The manager told her that today she had 17 rooms to clean and that she could take her lunch break when she wanted. She went to the tool room and gathered her cart and cleaning supplies to start her day. Her youngest daughter was home with a fever, so she first made a call to see if she were OK. She had her first child when she was only 12-years old. Fortunately, her children were all born in the United States and therefore U.S. citizens, although the current president was trying to stop this. Her niece made it across the Rio Grande River just in time to give birth on the U.S. side of the border, giving her son U.S. citizenship. No other country did such a stupid thing she thought, giving you citizenship just because you cross a river.

Reaching her fifth room and almost ready for a break, she stopped and pulled out an old transistor radio already tuned to her favorite Mexican radio station. She began humming to the song being played while knocking on the door announcing her presence. The room still stunk of cigarette smoke although the ashtrays on both nightstands were clean. The bed sheets had been disturbed, but not much. Sometimes she was tempted to just make up the bed with the existing sheets and call it done; most customers would probably never notice.

She pulled the sheets off the bed and threw them in her cart, then made up the bed with fresh linens. She quickly vacuumed the room and moved into the room she hated to clean the most--the bathroom. *Some people are complete slobs*, she thought while carrying her plastic bucket with cleaning supplies. At first glance it seemed that the prior occupants had left something inside the shower based on what she could initially see through the frosted glass. As soon as she rolled the glass door back she panicked and made the sign of the cross. "Oh, sweet Jesus," she said while making the sign of the cross. There, lying with her back against one of the walls was a nude woman whose head was resting on her chest, lifeless, bathed in the blood that also covered the shower floor.

Upon being notified, Maria Ruiz's manager immediately called 9-1-1, and after what seemed to take forever, the SFPD arrived at the scene. Forty minutes later, homicide detectives Tom Watson and partner Steven Andrade arrived at the motel as well. After checking the crime scene and talking with CSI, they went to the office to meet with Mrs. Ruiz and the manager. They examined the motel registration card and found Daniel Koufax's signature, and sure enough, a review of the security tapes showed Koufax entering the motel room with his victim. Koufax actually looked at the camera and smiled.

CHAPTER 15

Jeannie found a letter from the Marin County Sheriff's Department lying on her desk when she came back from lunch. It was addressed to the "Task Force Leader" at the Sheriff's Department. Having no idea of the contents, she put on a pair of latex gloves. It was a printed letter, several pages in length. *It began,*

"Hello Agent Loomis, How is my favorite FBI agent? This is Joey. Do you miss me?" Jeannie could feel her pulse increase and bile rise in her throat.

"Sorry for the loss of your fellow agent, Pinheiro. It was never the intention of the Sons

and Daughters of Liberty, nor me, to declare war on police. But, like all wars, there will

always be collateral damage. I saw you on television and want to congratulate you on

being chosen as the task force leader on the Koufax serial killing investigation. I hope you are more successful in catching him than you have been in locating me." *You prick*, Jeannie thought.

"Soon an event will take place that will have society totally forgetting all about Mr. Koufax and his infamous deeds. My event will make it in all the history books, although our socialistic education system does not teach history so most people will have to hear about it on social media.

I wanted you, Agent Loomis, to be the first person to understand the justification for my action. The United States, America if you will, that I took an oath to defend, is becoming a Marxist state. Every day the radical left chips away at our freedom. If you do not believe me, just look at what is happening in those cities governed by the Democrats. Cities like Los Angeles, San Francisco, Philadelphia, Chicago, Minneapolis, and one of the worst, New York. Even the capital of our U.S. government, Washington D.C., has become testaments to the workings of the Marxist left.

Where Democratic members of Congress and the liberal press glorify MS-13 as just normal 'gang members' who hold jobs and go to school. They downplay the atrocious acts of violence these hoodlums part take in, when in fact, they are an international criminal organization.

To me, the last straw was when I heard of a pending bill in Congress called The New Way Forward Act. Are you, Agent Loomis, aware of this bill? Assuming you are not since you are busy chasing me and Mr. Koufax, I will fill you in. The media, by the way, has given this bill no publicity. They do not want Americans to know about it.

It is sponsored by forty-four House Democrats. It is approximately 4,400 words long, almost exactly the length of the U.S. Constitution. It is designed to create a whole new country. It would remake our immigration system specifically allowing criminals from other countries to move here in complete immunity. I am not exaggerating, Agent Loomis. You can look it up after you finish reading my letter.

It is the most radical piece of legislation that has ever been proposed in the history of the United States--ever. Convictions should not lead to deportation. The bill specifically addresses felony convictions, not jay-walking or petty theft--felonies. One representative even bragged about this law breaking the pipeline between prison and deportation, something most Americans are for. Crimes of moral turpitude, such as child molestation, are eliminated, totally, as justification for deportation. The category of aggravated felony also eliminated under this bill. Bottom line, under this bill no crimes, no matter how grievous, will allow a person to be deported.

If that is not enough, the bill gives judges the right to dismiss deportation requests simply on humanitarian purposes, whatever that means. This will allow anti-American magistrates, who disagree with deportation, to turn any and all deportation request down simply by saying no, if they disagree with the process.

Are you mad yet Agent Loomis? No? This bill states that immigrants desiring to enter the Unites States who have drug crimes or any moral turpitude charges, including sex with children, cannot be used to prevent their entrance over our borders. So, a drug cartel leader who is freed from prison in another country, say from Latin America, can waltz right into our country.

Speak out against this bill, and you are labeled a racist. It would pretty much eliminate ICE since they would be required to go before a magistrate and show that the individual they want to deport is a flight risk or has a history of violence, but this law prevents them from doing so. If this is not bad enough, this bill changes existing laws in America, by inventing a brand-new right. It is called the Right to Come Home. Can you believe it?

As I said before, but I must repeat, most Americans have never heard of this law due to our corrupt Marxist media outlets. Both parties are to blame. The Democrats do not want ma and pa at home to know what they are up to. The Republicans have no balls. They held all three Houses of Congress, yet never went after any of these left-wing radicals. They are all part of the system. A system that is broken. With the Democrats calling the shots, being backed by their cohorts, the press, and the Republicans only spouting hot air, the silent majority is once again stifled in their pursuit of freedom. That will soon change.

When you have a malignant tumor, you must cut it out. But if you are too late, the cancer will have already spread, like the situation we are facing as a nation. You cannot just eliminate a few politicians like we did with the judges of the Star Chamber. My message to the silent majority will be loud and clear. Wake up America. Take your nation back.

Glad I got that off my chest and I feel so much better knowing that you are now the first to understand the rational or motive for my big event. Again, sorry for your loss, but as Forrest Gump said, shit happens.

-Joey"

Jeannie returned the letter to its envelope and let the rage inside her fall before calling Darcy. She told Darcy about the letter and that she would be sending it to her for forensic analysis. They agreed that Joey was too intelligent to give up evidence, but they had to try. She asked if Ismail was around, but Darcy said she had not seen him. When asked how the case was going, Darcy said they had some really good leads they were following, and that it appeared the connection to the casino was, in fact, the Native American. "Tell Flores, to call me when he gets a chance," Jeannie said as she hung up.

Frank entered Jeannie's office and said, "We got another one."

"What? Where? When?" Jeannie asked.

"In your city, San Francisco. A maid found the deceased in a shower, and the SFPD confirmed it was our boy. I've already sent several teams to the crime scene, but the SFPD has two very competent detectives on the case. The prick even smiled at the security camera. I'm telling you, it's the end of the world."

"Where did that phrase come? Oh yeah, the old Alfred Hitchcock's movie, "The Birds." Take a look at this," Jeannie said as she handed Joey's letter to him with a pair of latex gloves. "I think that Joey's saying as much," she said.

"No, the phrase came from one of R.E.M's songs," Frank replied. He then sang the verse: "It's the end of the world as we know it."

"Oh, that's right. For some reason I was thinking of the old drunk at the Tides Bar and about his thoughts on why the birds in Bodega Bay were attacking humans," Jeannie said laughing. "God, we need to hurry up and catch this prick before I go crazy!"

"That's right. He was at the corner of the bar by himself, and the ornithologist was discussing the unlikelihood that different bird species would flock together, much less attack humans," replied Frank.

Jeannie smiled and raised her right hand with her cup of coffee above her head and said, "It's the end of the world, I tell you."

Virginia was irritated when her nephew came unannounced to her house expecting to be received with open arms and invited to stay the night. She always felt he had a screw loose when he was growing up, and now knowing he was a serial killer on the loose, she probably would not have hesitated to shoot him if she had a gun. Apparently feeling unwelcomed by his aunt, Koufax left after an hour with her. As soon as he departed, she quickly called the number she had seen on her television screen.

While wrapping up her morning briefing with the task force, Jeannie was notified by dispatch that a distant aunt of Koufax had just called on the task force hot line. Jeannie told everyone in the room to take a short break and that she would soon return to share new information. Jeannie and Frank entered the dispatch area where the tape had been rewound so they could hear it in its entirety.

"Hello, this is Mrs. Virginia Thorpe. Daniel Koufax is my nephew, the one you're looking for. He just left my residence about 5-minutes ago and is driving a small tan hatchback. I don't know the make or model, but it's not in good shape. He's driving toward Highway 101 and I don't know if he is going north or south once he gets there."

An APB (All Points Broadcast) was immediately initiated by Jeannie. Finally--a break in the case. Just like the movie "Highwaymen," someone gave Koufax up. One of the task force detectives, Sergeant Ron Adams, heard the broadcast and set-up on the entrance ramp to Highway 101 South. A few minutes later he saw a tan Ford Focus traveling in the middle lane. Sergeant Adams accelerated onto the freeway, but not so fast as to be detected, slowly weaving in and out of traffic until he was able to maneuver behind the vehicle and radio in the plates. Dispatch reported the vehicle was stolen and belonged to the homicide victim in San Francisco.

He then drove up alongside the passenger side door of the Focus, looking at the driver who stared ahead. Checking a recent photo of Koufax that he attached to his windshield visor, he made a positive identification and radioed it to dispatch, requesting back up. Soon he was joined by several CHP cruisers, several plain clothes units, and local patrol cars; two CHP and SFPD helicopters hovered above.

Many upcoming freeway exits had been blocked, and a CHP cruiser with emergency lights and siren activated was attempting to set up a traffic break. Detective Adams was weaving across all lanes rapidly, gradually slowing so that traffic stayed behind him. This was a common tactic used when there was an accident, a high-risk car stop, or a road hazard condition existed ahead. Stopping a serial killer qualified.

Jeannie and Frank joined the slow speed pursuit with Frank driving. It seemed like Koufax could care less about getting caught or had any fear of the law. He watched Detective Adams in his rearview mirror, yet did not accelerate. He had to know that the police had him. Even Detective Adams heard the pop, pop,

pop of helicopter blades cutting through the air above them. The slow speed pursuit continued, giving Jeannie and Frank a chance to catch up to the chase. At one-point Koufax gave Detective Adams the finger while looking in the mirror.

Quickly, Koufax cut across three lanes of traffic and took an open off-ramp, blowing through an intersection stop sign and forcing several cars off the road while increasing his speed. Officers had set up a roadblock several miles ahead, and threw down spike strips hoping to disable the vehicle. As Koufax rounded a turn, he saw the waiting patrol units. He accelerated and hit a spike strip, flattening all four tires; but he drove on--sparks flying and pieces of tire ripping off the rims. Koufax drove into the opposing lane of traffic nearly hitting a school bus, and finally lost control of the car, coming to a stop in the grassy median. He stayed in the vehicle.

Using his car's bullhorn, an officer ordered Koufax to roll down his window and place both hands outside. Eventually Koufax complied. He was instructed to open the door from the outside, still showing his other hand; the officers did not know if he had a weapon. He was ordered to come out of the vehicle with his hands in the air. He looked very upset, aggravated and defiant, and facing the reality that his crime spree was over, he fell to his knees without being ordered and laid on his stomach. Three uniformed officers slowly advanced on Koufax, and when they were only a few feet away he rolled onto his back and tried to take aim with a revolver. All three officers fired, hitting Koufax numerous times in the chest. After several months of a killing spree that spanned two states and resulted in the murder of seven women, Koufax was dead. Inside the vehicle they found the victim's purse and other feminine articles later traced to the others who fell for Koufax's charm: his trophies.

CHAPTER 16

The first thing Ismail said to Jeannie after she answered her cell was, "Hey boss, congratulations! Gee, after only a few weeks, you take a serial killer off the streets. I'm impressed!"

"Thank you, Ace. But I had a whole bunch of help on this one," Jeannie replied. "By the way, did Darcy tell you that Joey sent me a letter?"

"Yeah, I heard. What do you think he has planned?" Flores asked.

"God, who knows! I haven't had a lot of time to think about it, but now that Koufax is signed, sealed, and dead, I should be able to get back home and we can restart a workup on Joey, along with your casino caper. How is that going?" she asked.

"Pretty good, actually." Flores said. "I'm getting the feeling that things are slowing going our way. When do you think you'll have everything wrapped up over there?"

"Ah, you miss me," Jeannie said, laughing.

"No, I just need time to clean my stuff out of your office. You know, return the hot tub and flat-screen television," he replied.

"Very funny! I'll check in with Captain Gillman and see when he can spring me. This was never a who-done-it so his people should easily finish the post-arrest documentation and follow-up needs. There's no need for me to be here any longer. I've already released our agents, so they should be back in SF tomorrow morning. I'll give you a call once I know for sure. Say hi to your wife for me," she said as she hung up.

The briefing room was filled with high-fives and backslapping; a lot of hard work had finally paid off. Gillman had ordered twenty-five pizzas and tons of soda for the task force. Jeannie entered to enthusiastic applause and a warm handshake from Gillman. Some asshole started to chant "speech, speech," and Gillman waved his hand at Jeannie, giving her the floor.

Jeannie cleared her throat and looked at everyone, trying to establish brief eye contact with all present. "You all have selflessly given the task force everything you had. You kept long hours and worked weekends, and some of you worked round the clock. For that, I say thank you. Your efforts took a serial killer off the streets permanently." Shouts of joy filled the room. "Time caught up to Mr. Koufax. He lost the Time Game. So, enjoy this triumph of good over evil and have a great time, but I hope you'll do something when you finally get home. Give some love to your family and friends, since they've suffered right along with you in our efforts to bring an end to this killer. Finally, it was an honor working with each and every one of you; and if I may, I'd like to leave you with a short song made famous by one of American's great clowns, the late Red Skelton. And no, I'm not going to sing it."

"Why not? Come on, we can take it," someone yelled. Jeannie felt redness rise into her cheeks as she started to recite the verse.

"The time has come, to say goodnight, my how time does fly. We had a laugh, perhaps a tear, and now we say goodbye. I really hate to say goodbye for times like these are few. I really wish you happiness, in everything you do. The time has come to say goodnight and I hope I've made new friends. And so, I'll say, may God bless, until we meet again." With that, Jeannie dabbed tears from her eyes and said, "Thank you one more time." More applause filled the room.

Frank handed a plate of pizza to Jeannie who didn't realize until that moment how starved she was. "Ever think of become an actress?" Frank asked. "I think several of the males in the audience shed some tears with your farewell." He gave her a diet Dr. Pepper and the two of them followed Captain Gillman to his office.

"Jeannie, I don't think I can thank you enough for what you accomplished with the task force," he told her.

"Your men and women did the leg work. Frank and I just acted as quarterbacks. They deserve all of the credit," she replied while taking a sip of soda.

"That may be, but you took on a huge responsibility to help relieve the pressure on my heart caused by the stress of this investigation, and I'll never forget what you did. So now, what are your plans," he asked. Frank also waited for her response.

"Well, I'm glad you brought that up. Frank is aware that during this investigation an old nemesis sent me a letter. He was indirectly involved in Ricky's, I mean Pinheiro's murder. He's now threatening to do something to wake up America. He's very intelligent, and I'm afraid of what he might be planning. I was hoping to immediately turn the reins over to Frank here, and head across the Golden Gate to the bureau if you concur.

"I don't see any problem with that. Do you Frank?" Gillman asked.

"No. It was a justified shoot. The DA is satisfied. Hell, there was more than enough evidence against Koufax that the DA would have sought the death penalty; so as I see it, we saved taxpayers money. Since Koufax won't be talking, I doubt we'll ever learn who gave him shelter and aid during our search for him. If I need information about the case, I can just give Jeannie a call," Frank said as he smiled at Jeannie.

"Alright Jeannie. Take off whenever you're ready, and tell old Lomax that I'm really indebted to him big time," Gillman said as he offered Jeannie a handshake.

"Yeah, I agree with you about that not taking a knee before the National Anthem shit, Sam said to Joey over lunch from the roach wagon. Those son-of-a-bitches are all millionaires. Just because they can dribble a ball, knock some asshole to the ground or hit a curveball, they basically shit on the flag of the country that gave them their venue. If this shit keeps going, I won't be watching any sports in the future. Know what I mean?" he asked.

Joey agreed with Sam, but his mind was on installing the final device in the air conditioning unit he was working on. The next day he would bring in the canisters. He had rigged a silent cooling system for each unit to keep the virus cold until he sent the command for plungers to activate aerosols and spray their deadly mist into the crowd of Democratic attendees. The gas had no odor nor would it have any immediate effect on those he considered pieces of shit. No, they would go about their left-wing agenda and then take the virus to their offices and homes. The only caveat was that several security teams would inspect the auditorium the next day. He hoped his devices would go undetected. Then, safely out of the area, all he had to do was make a phone call.

CHAPTER 17

By the time Jeannie cleared out her temporary office at the Sheriff's department and said her goodbyes, it was late. She was contemplating another night in the cheap hotel room, but then realized she really wanted to sleep in her own bed, the bed she and Ricky shared. She swung by the hotel and convinced the night manager to close her account even though she was well past checkout time. Slyly displaying her FBI badge seemed to do the trick. She amused herself by thinking she hadn't really done it for preferential treatment--she just opened her wallet and for some reason the flap covering her badge lifted and displayed it.

Instead of rehashing the Koufax case, Jeannie found herself driving across the Dumbarton Bridge thinking about Joey. She had copies of his letter on her phone after requesting that Darcy send them to her. Before sending them, Darcy told Jeannie that nothing of evidentiary value was found on the document's surface. It looked as if Joey had made a copy of a copy to make sure nothing was left to be traced. Jeannie would transfer the document to her printer, enlarge it, and put it on her bedroom wall per her normal practice. She opened her garage door and parked the Vette inside. At this late hour she felt safe that she would not have a run-in with Delores. She closed the garage door and entered the house that still smelled of fresh paint, paint that Ricky had put on the walls they would be sharing--if Joey's SDL member had not killed him. Jeannie had no tears this time--only anger and the need for revenge.

Jeannie got up very early the next morning, not to just get to work early, but to avoid running into Delores. She showered, put her hair in a ponytail, placed her Glock in the holster and was on her way to the donut shop for a cup of coffee and cinnamon roll. There was an accident in the westbound lane of the Dumbarton Bridge, so her plan of getting to the bureau early backfired. She popped in the audiobook she wanted to finish: "*Hitting Rock Bottom*." Hearing stories of juvenile delinquents who most of society had given up on, and their transformations in a strict, by-the-book, military academy school was inspiring to her. *I wonder how Joey would have turned out if he had attended such an institution,* she thought.

By the time she reached her office floor and exited the elevator, nearly all of the agents who reported to her were at their stations. She checked in with her receptionist, grabbed her While-You-Were-Out notes, and headed toward her office where she dropped the notes on her desk, took off her blazer and proceeded to the breakroom. There she found a large cake with frosting spelling out "congratulations" and "welcome back," and several helium balloons tied to chairs surrounding the table. Ismail entered, acting as if he were totally surprised by the cake and balloons. Jeannie knew differently. That was one of the things she loved about Flores.

"About time you got back here and did some real FBI work," he said as he grabbed a cup of coffee and doctored it with sugar and coffee creamer. "Everything finished up in Marin County?" he asked while taking a seat.

"Yes, they just have a few things needing to be addressed. The shooting of Koufax was justified."

"Yeah, I remember Marsha Clark saying something like that in the O.J. trial," Ismail said while eyeing the cake. Soon several agents entered the room, including SAC Lomax and Jeannie's receptionist; the last to enter were Burk and Darcy. All offered Jeannie welcome back greetings and congratulations, and then she cut the cake into generous portions. As things started to wind down, Lomax asked Jeannie to follow him to his office. Jeannie thanked those who were still in the breakroom and followed Lomax, telling Ismail that she would catch up with him after her meeting.

"Got a call from Captain Jerry Gillman last night. He now owes me big time for your efforts running the task force. Thank you," Lomax said while taking a seat.

"As I told Jerry, the task force members did the work. I only acted in an advisory capacity," Jeannie said.

"That's not what I heard, but thank you anyway. OK, I understand that Joey is threatening some type of event. Any leads or ideas?" he asked.

"No. I 've gone over his letter several times, but nothing hints as to what he's up to. I hope to share the information with my team and see if we can split up our energies as we solve the casino robbery and try to decipher Joey's intentions."

"OK, but if you need more manpower speak up. Needless to say, I don't want any blowback if Joey's able to pull off an event. That psychopath scares me more than the jihadists."

"Will do, and thanks for recommending me to Jerry for the task force job."

"I didn't recommend you; Jerry specifically asked for you. I guess there's a rumor going around that you're a highly competent leader," he said with a soft smile on his face.

Jeannie saw Ismail in the hallway and motioned for him to meet in her office. "OK, let's start with your progress on the casino job. Where do we stand?" Jeannie asked while taking her seat.

"We just received a drawing made while our witness was under hypnosis. Here's your copy. The forensic artist feels the witness came up with a lot of detail while he was under. I know we can't use it in court, but we need any lead we can get."

Jeannie studied it for a few seconds and then returned her attention to Ismail. He continued, "He was only able to remember the letters of the plate, so that's not going to help us. I gave you what we have on the Native American; his personnel file had nothing. It wouldn't surprise me if the casino sanitized it before we hit them with the search warrant."

"OK, let me hold a press conference with the media and see if they will cooperate by showing the drawing to their viewers. Maybe we'll get lucky. It seemed to help the task force in Marin County."

Joey stood next to Sam, eating a breakfast burrito from the food truck, which due to the security detail at the auditorium, had to move one block down from its previous location. "Here come the K-9s," Sam said excitedly. "I wonder if they're going to find any bombs?" he said while wiping hot sauce off his face and laughing.

Joey laughed, but his attention was definitely on the dogs as they entered the large building with their handlers. Joey shook Sam's hand, saying goodbye and that he hoped to meet him again at other construction sites, then proceeding down the street to a pale blue Dodge van which he entered. He climbed to the rear, picked up a pair of binoculars and watched the security force going in and out of the complex. Thus far, they did not seem concerned, so the dogs were probably trained to search for explosives instead of viruses. *Two more days and America will wake up*, he thought.

CHAPTER 18

At 2 p.m. Jeannie held a news conference that provided a short synopsis of the robbery and a few tidbits about the investigation's progress, giving television stations enough time to edit, cut, and paste for their five o'clock broadcasts. She did not show them the drawing of Johnny Loma, not wanting the suspects to know that one of their members had been identified and that the noose was tightening; she did not want the composite drawing done under hypnosis to spook the group of robbers. *That should give the media enough to chew on. Let them do their own follow up,* she thought. At the conclusion of her presentation she allowed a brief Q & A session, and afterward she felt she had not given up too much information. Each reporter was given a copy of the artist's drawing, however.

She touched base with Ismail before heading home. She was feeling the effects of the Koufax investigation, knowing she was running on pure adrenalin; it had kept her going the past few days—that, and junk food she thought, catching a smile on her face. Now to go home, fill the tub with lavender bubble bath and maybe have a bottle of beer--just relax.

After stopping at the local Subway, she finally arrived at her house. The garage door did not open fast enough. Out of the corner of her eye she saw Delores jogging from her house to hers, and in tow was her husband, Walter, who had been entrusted with carrying their dog. *There's no doubt who wears the pants in that family*, Jeannie thought.

"Hi Delores. How have you been?" Jeannie asked before Delores could open her mouth.

"I should be asking you that, young lady. How are you, and before I forget--what did I say the other day on the phone that gave you inspiration about your serial killer case?"

Jeannie knew this was the actual motivation for Delores' sprint at Olympic speed from her house to Jeannie's. Poor Walter was out of breath and Jeannie could see he really wanted to give the dog to Delores to hold.

"Well, remember when you asked me if I had seen that movie, 'Highwaymen'?"

"That's a real good movie," Walter said. "It has Kevin Costner and Woody Harrelson in it." Delores gave him the evil eye and Walter went back to paying attention to the dog. "How did that help you?" Delores asked.

"Well, you pointed out that the two Texas Rangers were basically chasing Bonnie and Clyde, and the Burrow gang all over the place, and they were always one step behind. They then realized that they seemed to return frequently to their old haunts where relatives and friends provided them a safe haven, and that they knew the area well. So, with that thought in mind, my team focused on those areas that seemed to be visited the most by our suspect. Similar to the movie, many of his friends and relatives began feeling the heat we were putting on them, thus limiting the number of places our killer could utilize. Eventually, he was forced to contact other individuals who were not as loyal as his previous contacts. So, you two actually solved our case. Thank you so much."

"Wow! Can you believe that Walter?" an excited Delores said. "We helped the FBI catch one of the Ten Most Wanted. I can't wait to tell our neighbors. Oh, wait. Is it OK if I do that? I don't want to hurt your chances of convicting him in court--you know, with all those slimy defense attorneys and all."

"No, that would be OK. Mr. Koufax is faced with a lot of evidence against him, and we're fairly confident he's going away for a long time." Jeannie purposely yawned, while saying she was beat, and wanted to take a long bath and go to bed early. Delores either took the hint, or because of the time realized it would soon be too late, and she had so many houses to hit with the news that she helped solve a serial killer case.

She welcomed Jeannie home and quickly passed by Walter, yelling at him to hurry up and get the dog home. She had a lot of neighbors to visit and he was slowing her down.

Jeannie smiled and looking up to heaven, knowing that Ricky was rolling with laughter.

The next morning Jeannie felt rejuvenated. She made herself a big breakfast and checked her phone for messages. Finding none, her thoughts turned to Joey's letter. She transferred the data from her cell to her laptop, increased the font size and then sent it to her printer. Once the task was completed, she put the letter on the wall with a picture of Joey in the center. "OK, you fucker." she said. "What are you trying to say? You're not as smart as you think you are. Eventually you're going to screw up and I'm going to get your ass."

As she read and re-read the letter, her phone rang. It was Ismail. "Hey, Ace. What do you have?" she asked.

"I have a body that women can't resist," he said.

"Oh God, spare me. It's too early. I really think you're suffering from a delusion of grandeur, my friend," Jeannie replied while trying to suppress a laugh. "How does your wife put up with you?"

"Hey, she knows how lucky she is," Ismail replied.

"You have any new information, or did you call just to inflate your ego?" Jeannie asked.

"Well, your presser yesterday may have paid off. An anonymous phone call came in about ten minutes ago from a female who gave the name of another female she claims knows about the robbery. I ran her name through the system, and we came up with a female who has a suspended license. I requested the South San Francisco Police, that's where she lives, to put a surveillance on her and to pick her up if they see her driving. She either owns or rents one of the houses you see on the hill when you drive to the city on Highway 101 from the airport--you know, they all look alike. Those houses inspired songwriter Pete Seeger to write "Little Boxes Made of Ticky-Tack." Anyway, just before I called you they informed me she's now in their custody awaiting you and me for a little meeting with her. When can you meet me there, so I can give them an ETA?"

Jeannie jumped into her Vetter and headed to the Dumbarton Bridge. The South San Francisco Police Department serves a population of over 60,000 residents and nearly 100,000 people who work there during the week. Located closer to the San Francisco International Airport than the City of San Francisco, many people traveling on Highway 101 don't even know that South San Francisco is not part of San Francisco proper. It is a small department of approximate 83 sworn officers, but for a small department compared to San Francisco, Jeannie had always been impressed with their training and professionalism.

When she pulled into the parking lot, she saw Ismail resting against his bureau car and holding two

Dutch Brothers coffee cups. "The sergeant told me she's scared and confused, and is asking why she's being held just for driving to work. She apparently feels that driving is a right, and just because her license is suspended it doesn't give the police the right to arrest her. Also, they warned me that she's a third-year law student and expects respect," Ismail said. "I knew that was going to impress you."

"Just what we need, another fucking lawyer," Jeannie said as they walked toward the police building. After identifying themselves, the two were escorted into the investigation division where they met Lieutenant Thomas Jackson. Jeannie told Jackson why they wanted to interview the arrestee and he directed them to a small interview room. They entered the room, finding an extremely skinny Black female who appeared to have lost the battle against acne when she was a child since her forehead and cheeks were covered with scars.

Jeannie had been given the woman's suspended driver's license by Lt. Jackson, and after glancing at the license addressed the arrestee. "Ms. Mays, I'm Special Agent Jeannie Loomis and this is my partner, Special Agent Ismail Flores. Should I call you Ms. Mays or would it be OK to call you by your first name, Sylvia?"

"I don't give a damn what you call me. I want to know why I'm being harassed for simply driving on a suspended license. I know the law and you can't keep me here. You're violating my civil rights."

"Well, we know the law also since combined we have over 30-plus years in law enforcement, but we're not here to discuss the issue of whether a driver's license is a privilege or a right," Jeannie said. "But, since I know you're a successful law student, I believe you know that lying to a federal agent in itself, is a felony. In addition, withholding information on a felony would come under the impending an investigation statue. You're aware of that, aren't you?"

Jeannie's technique of first complimenting Mays for being a successful law student and then insinuating that Mays could be in a lot of trouble, threw Sylvia off her game. "Ms. Mays, it has been brought to our attention that you have information regarding the recent casino robbery. And, before you say 'you don't know anything,' let me point out that three security guards were killed as a direct result of that robbery. This means that those involved could be facing the death penalty if convicted. Of course, you are aware of that." Jeannie paused to let Mays process everything.

"OK, I think my partner has spelled out the consequences for not cooperating with us, so now I'll give you a direct question. What do you know about the casino robbery?" Flores asked.

"Mays eyes teared up and she wiped them on the sleeve of her blouse. "I don't know anything about the robbery," she said, but before Jeannie and Ismail could object, she continued, "but I know someone who does. My friend, Kathleen Espinosa called me after watching television where they showed a photograph of one of the robbers. The news station gave an overview of the armored car robbery and then ended by asking for help in identifying the person in the picture. Espinosa told me that she suspected her boyfriend was involved." After making Mays repeat her story twice, she was asked about the location of Espinosa. Mays gave Jeannie and Ismail the name and address of the company where she worked.

After watching the security detail enter and leave the auditorium for hours, Joey was satisfied that his planted devices had not been discovered. He looked at his wristwatch and determined that only 72-hours remained before a filled arena would inhale the deadly vapor.

CHAPTER 19

They left Jeannie's Vette at the South San Francisco Police Department lot and went together in Ismail's Crown Vic. Espinosa was the assistant manager at a payday loan company located in a small strip mall. Borrowers visit a store like this and secure a small cash loan, with payment due in full when the borrower gets their next paycheck. The borrower writes a postdated check to the lender in the full amount of the loan plus outrages fees.

"You know, in the old days the rates this firm charges would be considered loan sharking," Ismail said as he found a parking space near the firm's entrance.

"You sound like you're in a bad mood. What happened? Did your wife have enough of you and make you sleep on the couch where you read Wikipedia before falling asleep?" Jeannie asked as she got out of the car.

"Funny! Very funny," Ismail said as he put on his suit jacket, covering his weapon.

When they entered, they saw a male teller behind a small counter talking to a customer. To his right was a very small office where a smartly dressed female was working, but glanced up when they entered. She left her office and approached Jeannie and Ismail.

"Hello, how may I help you? she asked.

"We're looking for Kathleen Espinosa," Ismail said as both he and Jeannie showed their identification.

"I'm Kathleen Espinosa. Has something happened?" she asked, turning a bright shade of red.

"Can we speak to you in your office?" Jeannie asked.

"Sure, please," Espinosa replied, pointing to her office and leading the way. "What's this all about? I'm so nervous."

While driving to Espinosa's place of employment, Jeannie and Ismail discussed how they wanted to handle the interview. It was decided that this time Ismail would be the good cop, while Jeannie played the baddy. Before starting the interview, Jeannie explained the nature of their investigation and the pitfalls that could happen if Espinosa refused to cooperate, lied, or interfered with the case. She made sure to emphasis that failing to answer questions truthfully was a federal charge in itself. Espinosa began to cry; she knew why the FBI were in her office. She agreed to answer the agent's questions and opened up voluntarily.

"My boyfriend, Alan Page, asked me one night what I would do if he held up an armored car and suddenly had a lot of money? He sometimes works as a bounty hunter and is usually broke. On the day of the robbery he told me he had killed someone and had a lot of cash on him. I thought he was joking, but he told me he was telling the truth. Like I said, he sometimes does bounty hunting with his friend, Billy Ring."

"What type of cars do your boyfriend and this Billy Ring have?" Ismail asked.

"Alan has a Harley and Billy has a red truck," she replied.

Jeannie and Ismail glanced at each other hoping this was the red rust colored truck they were looking for. "What does Billy Ring's truck look like?" Jeannie asked.

"Oh, it is not new or anything. The paint's faded and there are a lot of dents in it," Espinosa answered. "Anyway, a few days after the robbery Page and I went to Ring's residence and found several new ATVs, jet skis, and dirt bikes. Ring told her she would never be able to guess the amount of money in his garage."

Jeannie knew the information Espinosa was providing was good, but it was only hearsay. They needed more solid evidence. Almost on cue as if she read Jeannie's mind, Espinosa grabbed her purse, stopped, looked at both Ismail and Jeannie, and asked if she could get something out of her purse. "Slowly," Jeannie said and both she and Ismail placed their hands on their weapons.

Espinosa pulled five rolls of coins from her purse, mostly quarters, and placed them on her desk. Ismail picked up the roll of coins and saw they were marked similarly to rolls of coins found scattered in the back of the armored van. Espinosa was warned not to reveal their discussion or face being charged with an accessory after the fact. She explained that she had some saved vacation time and would fly to Texas and visit her family so she could avoid her boyfriend, if that were permissible. Jeannie told her it would be, but asked if she had a passport. She denied having one. Ismail asked for the address where she would be staying in Texas as well as her cellphone number.

Jeannie contacted Darcy while walking back to Ismail's car, asking her to make sure Espinosa did not have a passport. Darcy was able to quickly confirm that she did not.

It was getting close to lunchtime after they wrapped up their interview with Espinosa, so they picked up fast-food and headed to the bureau. Most of Jeannie's other agents assigned to the casino heist were in the breakroom. "Got some solid leads on the case everyone," Flores said while taking a seat. "We now know the names of three suspects," and he began naming them.

"Billy Ring? I know that asshole," Agent Scott O'Flannery said. "I've used him in the past as an informant in some investigations. He used to be a prison guard down in Phoenix, if I remember correctly."

Darcy and Burk entered the room carrying salads. "Are we having a party or what?" Burk asked. "Actually, I'm glad you two are here," Jeannie said. "We have two more individuals to workup. Scott just told us that one of them, a Billy Ring, used to be a prison guard in Arizona. Can you get on it right away? Let's meet in the briefing room in an hour and see where we are. I think we're close, very close," Jeannie said as she grabbed her soda and headed to SAC Lomax's office to give him an update on the case.

Joey was in his motel room in the city of Brisbane, several miles from the San Francisco International Airport. Bored out of his mind with nothing to do but wait until the big event night, he got a smile on his face, and picked up his gloves and rental car keys. *She shouldn't be home and it has been a long time since my last visit*, he thought while he whistled "I Shot the Sheriff "on the way to his car.

CHAPTER 20

After bringing Lomax up to speed, Jeannie checked in to see if she had any messages. Frank Gilman from the Marin County Sheriff's Department said to give him a call, but stressed that it was not urgent. *What the hell?* she thought; she had a little time before going back to the briefing room.

"Hi, Frank. It's Jeannie. You called?"

"Hey, you. I just called to let you know that Washoe County, Nevada, found another body that we think matches the Koufax M.O. She went to a bar the night of her disappearance and hadn't been seen since. The body's in pretty bad shape due to decomposition, but all the circumstantial evidence points to him. Their investigators will try to track down as many customers that frequented the bar as possible, and do the same follow-up we did. With what Koufax is already facing, what is one more, right? Any progress on the Joey case?" Frank asked.

"No, all we have is his letter right now, and our main focus has been on that casino robbery/homicide case. We feel that one is about to break."

"Hey, we need all the breaks we can get. OK, I won't keep you--just wanted to keep you in the loop. Take care and stay safe." With that, they hung up.

SAC Lomax attended Jeannie's briefing that afternoon. Darcy started with overhead slides of the three known robbery suspects: Billy Ring, Alan Page and Johnny Loma. She confirmed that both Page and Ring had worked for the Phoenix Department of Corrections and had many hours of firearm training before they were terminated for becoming too close to prisoners. "Now get this," Darcy said. "Loma also had a license as a part-time bounty hunter. If we can connect the dots, Loma must have told Page and Ring about the upcoming poker tournament. People at the prison remember Ring as being the stronger of the two, and that Page looked up to him.

Burk and I think that Loma, Page, and Ring came up with the plan to rob the armed car, but they realized it would take at least four people to pull it off. O'Flannery pulled his old records on Ring and found a note that his stepbrother was Roy Barr, an ex-con having done time for bank robbery. He's a possible suspect."

Ismail jumped in saying, "That makes sense. With Ring, Page and Loma being bounty hunters, they are aware of police tactics such as surveillance techniques. When we find these guys, we'd better be ready."

"Jeannie," Burk said. "These are the addresses Darcy and I found on all the suspects." Jeannie immediately ordered both ground and air surveillance of all three suspects.

"Darcy, you and Burk focus on their bank accounts. Check to see how they've been earning and spending money. To my knowledge only Loma had a steady income, coming from his employment at the casino. I want to know if they have any part-time jobs or if they're all collecting unemployment benefits. The witnesses Ismail and I talked to said they're all spending a lot of cash.

Terry, I want you and Mary to contact all the local ATV, jet ski, and motorcycle shops in their immediate area and see if any of them have been doing business, and if so, are they paying only in cash--which I suspect they are. I'll bet they're staying under the $10,000 limit to avoid the IRS. The rest of you will be assigned surveillance duty. I want to monitor these guys 24/7, so if you think you'll need more manpower to make this happen, contact me. Better prepare your families; this may take some time. Alright, let's hit it," Jeannie said as she turned and left the briefing room.

Shit, that Goddamn nosy bitch neighbor always seems to be outside talking to someone, Joey thought to himself, as he watched Jeannie's home from a block away. *That old busybody sure covers a lot of ground.*

Maybe I should get something to eat and come back later, which he did.

Joey found a McDonald's less than a half-mile away, and after using the drive-thru he parked under a shade tree to enjoy his meal. He found himself speaking to the car radio, agreeing and disagreeing with the talk show host. "Now these assholes are tearing down statues of everyone that doesn't fit their ideological narrative, supported by the democrats and indirectly by the damn GOP who doesn't speak out on the issue. You motherfuckers will pay in a few days," he muttered.

Joey drove through Jeannie's neighborhood again, but the "bitch" was still out talking to neighbors. He really did not want to return across the bay to his motel room after coming all this way.

It was such a nice day, Joey decided to visit the Tideland Trail located about 1 mile from Jeannie's residence. He saw a brochure about it laying on a table inside the fast-food restaurant. He turned right onto Marshlands Road, left his rental car in the parking lot, and started walking the 0.7 mile paved trail that traversed through uplands, tidal slough, salt pond, and tidal salt marsh. A sign informed visitors that the Tideland Trail was the home to shorebirds and grebes that were plentiful in the pond during the winter. *That's interesting if a person knew what a damn grebe was*, Joey thought while laughing to himself.

He was able to waste almost forty-minutes on the trail and hoped that by that time Jeannie's Gestapo neighbor was inside her house. Entered the neighborhood, he felt he had lucked out; she was nowhere in sight. He parked around the corner near a sign stating that the subdivision was protected by Neighborhood Alert, put on the hard hat and tool belt he'd used in the auditorium, and walked toward Jeannie's house carrying a clipboard and a few blank pieces of paper. *It's amazing*, he thought, *how people wearing worker's clothes and carrying a clipboard seem to go unnoticed in most neighborhoods. This one should be no different.*

Well, Agent Loomis, I hope you haven't installed a new alarm systems since my last visit, Joey thought as he picked the lock on the side door leading to the garage. *No, doesn't look like it.* He entered the empty garage and found the door leading from the garage to the kitchen unlocked. *Jeannie, Jeannie.... you should always lock all your doors*, a smiling Joey thought to himself as he entered her home.

Joey cautiously listened while standing in the kitchen, hearing no noise but noticing the smell of fresh paint. *Are you a DIY person Agent Loomis*? He knew from a past visit that there was nothing of interest downstairs, so he slowly climbed the stairs leading to the three bedrooms. He entered the master bedroom and could not resist going through the dresser drawers, finding Jeannie's sexy underwear and nightgowns. He smelled the underwear and smiled. *Not too kinky. Looks like either Victoria Secrets or Fredricks of Hollywood. Red and Black, my favorite colors,* he thought as he put the underwear back as he found them.

The second bedroom had several drop cloths on the floor and resealed paint cans in addition to two paint rollers, clean pans, and a roll of painting tape. Joey found nothing of interest there and continued his inspection. “Ah-ha,” he said in a whisper as he entered the third bedroom. “I see you’re still up to your old habits, Jeannie.” Joey found a bedroom wall covered with photos of individuals with their biographic information listed below. Several appeared to be security guards. There were pictures of a burned armored van in what appeared to be a canyon, as well as the picture of a casino.

Jeannie, you and your team are working the Indian Casino caper, huh? I’m disappointed. No pictures of me? Oh wait, I’m sorry; this wall has my letter displayed. You do think of me, Joey thought as he began reading his letter to himself.

He could not resist: he found a pen on a desk and walked up to the pictures of his letter. “Gee, I wish I could be here to see your face when you find my handwriting,” he said, as he completed writing a short sentence on the final page.

CHAPTER 21

At the following morning's briefing, Jeannie asked her team for an update. Surveillance teams had witnessed the known suspects meeting at various restaurants, and on one specific night, spending a lot of cash--unaware their every move was watched and recorded. Suspect number four, ex-con Roy Barr, had shown up at a strip club. Jeannie told everyone to keep it up. Darcy and Burk would be serving their search warrants at various banks later that morning and afternoon.

At the conclusion of the briefing, Jeannie headed back to her office, only to be told by her receptionist that she had just gotten off the phone with a person who said he had information about the robbery/homicides, but that he wanted to speak with Jeannie only. She called the number on the note given to her and asked for a Rocky Stewart. When the call ended, she immediately contacted Ismail.

"You know you're going to have a great day when you head back to your office and find a While-You-Where-Out note, and it turns out that the caller's a sour puss looking for revenge," she told Ismail as he entered her office. "Get this," she said. "A guy by the name of Sal (Rocky) Stewart wants to meet with me here at the bureau to tell what he knows about the robbery and killings. All he told me on the phone was that he was there when it was being planned, but he never took part in it. "He should be here within the hour, so make sure you're available."

Rocky Stewart was an obese heavily tattooed outlaw motorcycle thug. Jeannie escorted him to a small interview room where Ismail was already seated. She introduced Flores and thought that Steward might object to his presence, but he didn't.

"I was casing armored cars with both Ring and Page, you know--the routes, schedules and so on. We thought we had a choice target, but then the Indian told us about all this money coming to the casino. They were going to have a hell-of-a poker tournament and needed millions of dollars for prize money."

"Do you know the Indian's name?" Jeannie asked.

"Yeah, it's Johnny Loma, but I just call him Crazy Horse."

"Let me cut to the chase and ask why you're giving up this information?" Ismail asked.

"Those fuckers cut me out of the deal. What'd they get, twenty-five million? And what did I get? Nothing man. I mean, I was scouting out suitable targets with them and Johnny redskin comes in and steals my share. I mean all of a sudden, they give me the cold shoulder and invite Ring's step-brother, Ron Barr, into the group. I want those fuckers to burn. Serves them right for dropping me for the prick, Barr."

Jeannie thought of the old saying, "There's no honor among thieves."

"Why don't you give me all their names again so we can make sure we get them right," Ismail requested. Stewart leaned forward and watched Ismail write each one down on a yellow note pad. Seeing all their names correctly listed, Stewart crossed his arms and leaned back in his chair with a look of satisfaction. "You two have to make them pay for what they did to me."

Late that night the surveillance team watching Loma's residence felt it was time to do a little dumpster diving. In his trash placed curbside earlier by an unknow female, they found a torn map. They gathered the matching pieces of paper and took them back to the bureau. They showed them to Jeannie and instantly Burk and Darcy jumped at the task of putting the "puzzle" together. Taped back together, the map showed the canyon leading to the casino with an X where the tractor-trailer jackknifed. This information was shared with the rest of Jeannie's team the next morning.

All surveillance teams agreed that since the four suspects routinely met at Page's residence, the legal department had more than enough evidence to secure a search warrant granting bug placement inside. Ismail and Jeannie were in a car down the street from Page's residence waiting for the go-ahead to enter the house and place monitoring devices. As soon as Page left and they received the all clear sign, they headed toward his home. Jeannie pulled out her lock picks and went to work. In no time, she was able to defeat the lock and open the door. *Thanks for teaching me how to do this, Dad*, she thought as she slowly opened the front door. Immediately, an alarm went off. The two quickly hurriedly back to Jeannie's car and they left the area. "Shit!" Jeannie said, "We need an alarm expert to tag along with us. Do you know anyone?" she asked.

The two returned to Page's house in a van two hours later. This time they were accompanied by Jimmy Jenson (J.J.), a former agent with the NSA (National Security Agency) and a friend of Ismail's. As Jeannie opened the side door, the alarm went off again. Jenson quickly realized it was a simple motion detector and not a sophisticated device at all. He simply turned it off.

Jason, Ismail, and Jeannie began planting bugs in the front room, bedroom, and kitchen. When they were only half done, Jeannie got an alert from one of the surveillance teams that Page had just left a bar and appeared to be heading home. Jeannie did not want to make a return trip to the house, so she contacted the

CHP (California Highway Patrol) and asked them to pull Page over and caution him about speeding. That, she felt, would give them adequate time to complete the bug planting task. Fifteen-minutes after they left Page's residence, he pull into his driveway.

The next morning all four suspects met at Page's residence. While seated in a construction van two-blocks away, Darcy and Burk were busy recording information detected by the various room monitoring devices. The four discussed all the news updates about the robbery, laughing about what was accurate and what was not, and whether the FBI were on the right track. Unfortunately, there were no actual confessions. However, there was a considerable amount of circumstantial and general information about the crime, but still not enough to merit arrest warrants.

"Those assholes are either smart or just overly cautious. We need to turn up the heat and apply some pressure," Jeannie said to her agents after listening to the recording at the bureau. She then shared her thoughts about possible next moves.

One of Jeannie's ideas was immediately executed. She asked one of the surveillance team members to put her business card on Barr's front door when he was away. There was no message on the card, just the card itself. Two hours later the surveillance team announced that Barr had just arrived home on his Harley. As soon as he found the business card, he jumped back onto his bike and drove to an area near the Golden Gate Bridge and phoned Page. The monitoring equipment picked up their conversation.

"The FBI's on to us, dude. I just got home and there was a business card on my front door. No, there's no note, only the card with a Special Agent Jeannie Loomis's name on it," he was overheard saying while being monitored by Ismail, Jeannie, Burk and Darcy.

"Fuck it! I'm not going back to the joint. I'll commit suicide before that happens, I'm telling you man." Ring was finally able to calm down his stepbrother. A calmer Barr was overheard saying that if he saw one more cop, he was going somewhere and bury the money--a direct reference to the crime.

Jeannie saw Agent O'Flannery walking toward the breakroom. "Hey Tim. Got a minute?" she asked.

"You said you used Barr as a snitch in the past. What do you think about calling him in to the bureau under the guise that you want him to check out some photos of possible suspects in the armored car heist? Bring up about how valuable he had been to you as an informant in the past and build up his ego. If he agrees, let us know what time he'll be here so at the same time we can take down Loma, Page, and Ring. That way, they can't alert each other."

"Hey, that's one hell of a plan. I'll call him now," O'Flannery replied as he hurried off to a secure room to make the call.

"Ron, my main man, how's it going? This is Agent O'Flannery. How have you been? How's my star confidential informant? I see you've not gone back to the joint. I bet you're glad about that, huh? Congratulations."

Initially, Barr was hesitant to say anything to O'Flannery, until he told Barr that he needed his help again regarding the Indian casino robbery. "We've got some pictures of people we think might have been involved and hope that maybe you can recognize someone. I don't expect you to do this for free. I've got some bucks for your effort."

Either the ego stroking or curiosity of learning what the FBI had on the case, Barr agreed to come in and look at the pictures. He would be at the bureau in 30-mnutes, plus or minus. O'Flannery informed Jeannie that Barr was on his way.

Quickly, Jeannie arranged to have several of the FBI's arrest technique agents in the lobby of the bureau. Two were reading magazines and the third was playing with his cell phone, sitting next to a female agent using a laptop. At almost the 30-minute mark, Barr walked in. He glanced at the others in the room and then approached the receptionist. "I'm here to see Agent O'Flannery," he said.

"And your name sir?" the receptionist asked.

"I'm Ron Barr. He's expecting me."

Barr did not notice the men moving toward him until it was too late. On cue, three male tactical officers grabbed each of Barr's arms and took him to the ground. He did not resist. He was escorted downstairs to a small interview room. It appeared to the arresting agents that Barr knew he had walked into a trap. Jeannie requested O'Flannery and his partner, Agent Carol Salazar, a ten-year veteran with the FBI, to conduct his interrogation, while Darcy and Burk listened from their office.

Initially, Barr did not raise his head when the two agents entered the room; he kept his head down, avoiding eye contact. Mr. Barr, I am Special Agent Salazar. I know you're already acquainted with Agent O'Flannery, here. Why don't we start by you telling us all about the casino robbery.robbery? At this point, Barr finally lifted his head and looked, first at O'Flannery and then at Salazar. O'Flannery expected Barr to start out with a few expletives in disgust for being conned into coming the FBI office, but instead he appeared to give in to the inevitable.

"If I cooperate, can I cut a deal?" he asked.

"Ron," O'Flannery started, "You know you'll be going back to prison. The only thing that you can do in your favor is to cooperate. The last thing we want is for someone to get hurt or killed. It's over. We already know who was involved with you in the robbery. But we want to hear it from your lips. Our report will go to the prosecution office and we'll indicate that you were very instructive in helping us bring this case to a close.

Barr leaned forward, placed his arms on the table and interlaced his fingers. “Where do you want me to start?” he asked.

CHAPTER 22

While Barr was being taken into custody at the bureau, Jeannie, Ismail, and several of Jeannie's other agents executed search warrants simultaneously at the Barr, Page, and Loma residences. Finding any remaining money would be great, but she also told her agents to be alert for anything related to the robbery. "There's never too much physical evidence," Jeannie told her team the night before the raids.

As soon as Jeannie was notified that Barr had been taken into custody, she ordered the other three teams to execute search warrants on their respective targets. She and Ismail hit Page's house with four tactical officers, finding it vacant. The tactical squad was released and Jeannie requested that the forensic team enter the residence. After only a few minutes, the newest member of the forensic team called Jeannie to join her in Page's spare bedroom. She handed Jeannie a yellow note pad that had the initials "L," "B," and "R," with dollar amounts next to each.

Ismail, looking over the forensic team members shoulders and seeing the dollar amounts, pulled out his cellphone, quickly calculating the total which corresponded to the money taken in the heist. Jeannie and Ismail concluded that the letter "L" stood for Loma, "B" for Barr, and "R" for Ring. There was no "P" listed, but an easy subtraction indicated that Page took an equal share of the loot. An older, beat up red rust colored truck was found in the garage under a tarp, similar to the one used in the robbery and described by the witness who was out walking his dog. However, the license plate numbers did not match what the witness was able to recall under forensic hypnosis. "They must have been switching plates," Ismail said.

A .22 revolver and a duffle bag containing over $5 million dollars in cash was found in a garage wall stuffed under fiberglass insulation.

Similar results from the other three search warrant executions were reported to Jeannie. Loma seemed to be the most fugal of the four; almost all of his share was still accountable and still had the cash bands around each bundle of currency. His mobile home was also Spartan-like. Jeannie and Ismail surmised he was waiting for things to totally cool off before spending any of the money.

Barr, Page, and Ring appeared to have spent a lot of their shares. Barr had a flat-screen television in each of his bedrooms as well as both bathrooms. Each of the three had a new ATV, jet skis, and motorcycles in their possession. Ring seemed to have a fancy for designer clothes as well as having a collection of vintage Fender guitars.

During the following morning brief, Darcy and Burk determined that over $175,000 was missing from the robbery total, presumably spent by the four suspects. The case against the four seemed solid, but Jeannie hoped that playing the four off against each other might cause someone to turn. That person was Johnny Loma.

Loma refused an attorney after being advised of his Miranda Warning. For some reason the Johnny Cash tune "The Ballad of Ira Hayes" was in Ismail's head as he and Jeannie started their interrogation. Loma said that Page was the mastermind of the entire robbery. He, along with Barr and someone called Rocky had been watching the movement of several armored cars for several weeks. After learning that the casino was going to host a poker championship worth millions, and that the money had to be transported from the Federal Reserve, Page decided this would be the target. Loma kept an open ear around the casino where he worked and learned the date and time of the delivery, thinking it would be a simple takedown and that no one would be hurt, especially with the canyon layout the armored vehicle had to take. He said that Page and Barr decided to send the van over the cliff after they disabled all the guards; they didn't want anyone killed. When the four learned later that day from the media that the three security guards died, all were in shock, especially Barr. In an attempt to keep Barr from freaking out, Page told him that in all tactical situations there might be collateral damage, but since they pulled it off with such military precision, they would not get caught.

Loma's description of the planning, execution, and aftermath of the robbery/homicide was backed up by forensic evidence. He showed Jeannie and Ismail the suspects' positions when the armored vehicle arrived, as well as where they split up, burned the evidence, and agreed to meet later. When confronted with Loma's confession, Barr also rolled over and stated that they never intended to seriously hurt the guards. Page and Ring refused to waive their rights.

The next morning, SAC Lomax assembled all of the agents that had contributed to the successful culmination of the case in the larger briefing room. When the agents, including Jeannie and Ismail, entered they found a catering service waiting with a full breakfast menu. "Alright!" Ismail said, who became the first person in line. Jeannie walked up to Lomax and thanked him. "Don't get used to it," he replied while directing her to the buffet line. "We better get there quick, or Flores will eat everything," he said, laughing and staring at Flores.

"Forty-eight hours left," Joey said to the television screen in his motel room. The talking heads were discussing the big event in two days and showed pictures of arriving Democratic power brokers. Private Jeannie, jets were seen arriving at the Los Angeles International Airport and the congressmen and women were identified as they waved at the crowd. *Hey, I thought you assholes were all for the Green New Deal. Those plans didn't fly on electricity, you bastards. Why didn't you fat asses walk?* These and other thoughts ran through Joey's mind as the television scanned the large auditorium that would host the Democratic National Convention. As Joey recognized those he had total contempt for, the voice in his head became a little louder until he realized he had to remain cool.

After Lomax had eaten, he formally congratulated all the agents assembled for a job well done, and then asked Jeannie to meet him in his office. She followed a few minutes later. "Thank you, sir, for the nice breakfast. I'm sure the team loved it," Jeannie said as she took a seat across from her boss.

"I had actually wanted to tell them to leave early today after tying up all loose ends, but we really need to turn our focus on Joey and whatever he's planning. Any ideas?" he asked.

"No. I keep reading his letter and come up with nothing. I feel there's something there, but with the casino robbery taking all of our energy, we can't see it. Maybe now we can put all of our focus on it and figure out what he's planning to do," she replied.

CHAPTER 23

Jeannie loved her drive home across the bay on some occasions. Tonight, it was exceptionally pleasant; the lights were on at the Giants stadium. *Guess they have a night game,* she thought. She grew up loving the San Francisco Giants and 49ers, watching games with her dad both while growing up and on big game events, like when they were playing against the damn Los Angeles Dodgers. The last few years, however, she boycotted both the MLB and NFL due to their politics, which conflicted with hers. Actually, after the first year of her boycott and the boycotting by many others nationally, the NFL really took it in their shorts financially. It looked like they had learned their lesson; but the very next year, they allowed players to take a knee during the National Anthem, and that did it for her. No more sports other than maybe the Olympics until that, too, becomes politicalized.

Even though the eastbound traffic was heavy on the Dumbarton Bridge, she rolled down the windows of her Corvette, took in deep breaths of the salt air, and relaxed. She had her radio turned in the KSFO 560 and was listening to the "Mark Levin Show." He also had a show on Fox News called "Life, Liberty & Levin" which she occasionally watched. Considering herself an Independent like her father, she found she was more closely aligned with the ideology of the GOP. Before she lost her dad, he made a point that John F. Kennedy would today espouse the ideology of the Republicans, yet he was a Democratic President before his assassination. The Democratic Party today appeared to have been hijacked by the radical left of the party and trying to slowly turn the nation into a Socialist-Marxist country. Gee, she thought, are students learning anything about U.S. and World History in school?

Not wanting to spend a lot of time fixing a meal, she stopped at a Safeway and bought a few items to make sandwiches at home. She hit the store's deli counter and bought a pint of potato salad that she would doctor up to make it taste like the salad her grandmother used to make. Her thoughts turned to those nights when she came home and found Ricky in the kitchen preparing a homemade meal for the two of them, feeling he would be proud of the way she and her team took down the robbery/homicide suspects and solved another major crime. *Not a bad two weeks, huh honey?* she thought. We took down a serial killer and then the whole armored car gang.

She made it into her garage and closed the door, avoiding her next-door neighbor. Of course, nothing would prevent her neighbor from coming over anyway and knocking on the front door. For now, she had some peace. She kicked off her shoes and placed her service weapon on the kitchen counter, then turned on her television set and switched to One American News Network. The news was dominated by the upcoming Democratic National Convention down in Los Angeles. Thank God they decided to hold it down there, she thought. The female anchor started her show with the headlines creeping underneath her picture stating:

Democrats beware –Backlash against leftist mob rule growing. Here's what polls show.

This ought to be interesting, she thought as she placed condiments on her French Roll piled high with turkey, salami, and swiss cheese. She grabbed a hard-boiled egg, red onion, and some sweet pickles and chopped them up, then mixing them into the store-bought salad. After placing a scoop of potato salad on a plate next to the sandwich and grabbing a can of diet Dr. Pepper, she headed toward her couch.

Americans are fed up and they are angry – increasingly, they will push back. The backlash has begun.

The professor being interviewed by a female anchorwoman talked about "Cancel Culture." Jeannie had no idea what this was referring to, but with events described by the professor she quickly understood its meaning. She hear him say, "The looting of neighborhoods, the defaming of our nation's history, the destruction of public monuments, attacks on the police, and the non-stop dishonesty of the liberal media and vilification of the sitting President, was cropping up in ways big and small, and it will grow."

Jeannie had heard bits and pieces of the insurrection taking place in some major cities, but she had been so preoccupied with the SDL and Joey, the death of Ricky, the serial killer task force and then the casino robbery investigation, that she had no time to follow the news. *Gee,* she thought to herself. *This sounds bad.*

"Americans are fed up and they are angry. Increasingly, they will push back; polling shows that the Democrat candidate's lead over the President is shrinking significantly as a result."

Most persuasive, Jeannie felt, was his final comment: "A new Monmouth poll showing that a great number of Americans, though supportive of police reform and conscious of our racial divide, have declining sympathy with the Black Lives Matter movement and the notion that racial prejudice is a major problem for the United States."

The television screen was then filled with films of various protests around the country demanding that communities "defund the police," even as shootings of children pile up in New York, Chicago, Atlanta and other liberal cities. "Jesus, what the hell is wrong with people?" she said to the television set.

The professor concluded with, "Americans are losing patience, for good reason. It is crazy that people are losing their jobs and reputations for comments or opinions expressed, in some cases decades ago. Americans are also losing patience with the blatant hypocrisy of the Left. Some things would be laughable, except they speak to a suffocating suppression of dissent. Scrabble eliminating 226 "offensive" words from its lexicon, 'To Kill a Mockingbird' and 'Huckleberry Finn' banned from schools, sports teams scrambling to change their 'insensitive' names, Princeton scrubbing its campus of President Woodrow Wilson, Ford employees demanding the carmaker quit making police cars, and on and on. Even George Washington has been targeted."

I'll bet Joey is loving this, Jeannie thought as she took two yawns as a sign to take a long hot shower and get some sleep. She grabbed her shoes and gun, and climbed the stairs to the master bedroom. She took off her clothes and wrapped herself in an over-sized bath towel, and after grabbing her nightwear, headed to the bathroom. For some reason her thoughts returned to her and Ricky's discussion about putting a hot tub in the backyard. Ricky pointed out that Delores, her nosy neighbor, might have a heart attack if she spied on them doing the nasty in the hot water. Ricky joked about Delores possibly running into her house and giving Walter a night he would not soon forget.

After finishing her shower and drying her hair, Jeannie decided to make sure she had locked the downstairs doors. Finding them secure, she climbed the stairs once again, but instead of entering the bedroom she decided give Joey's ominous letter one last read. Perhaps, she thought, that after she read the letter again, she would have an epiphany and solve the cryptic document while falling asleep.

As she turned on the light she saw markings on the document hanging on the wall. She sprinted to her bedroom, grabbed her Glock and quickly called 9-1-1. After identifying herself as an FBI agent, she requested that officers respond to her residence. She then called Ismail, who offered to come as well; but Jeannie said there was no need.

"What did his note say?" Ismail asked.

Jeannie approached the attached letter and read it to him:

"Hello Agent Loomis. Sorry I missed you again. I see you are doing some upgrading in your home.

I approve. I would have suggested a different color scheme, however. In just a few more days, the silent majority will be able to breathe a little easier. Those that I will eliminate will allow traditional, Constitutional loving Americans a chance to regroup and rectify the cancer the left has infected into our society in an attempt to cancel our culture. I am sorry that innocent blood will also be sacrificed, but it could not be helped. Hope to speak with you in the future. Thinking of you, Joey."

The local police arrived, and even though Jeannie told them her residence was secure, they inspected the premises, including the garage. It appeared that Joey had somehow defeated her alarm system--something she would have to discuss with her service provider later. A forensic team arrived and took a lot of prints, but Jeannie was not expecting them to find anything. She thanked them for their response.

CHAPTER 24

Jeannie arrived at the bureau shorty after Ismail and together they took the elevator to Jeannie's floor. "That fucker was in my house again," she said. "How did the bastard defeat my alarm system?" Ismail did not offer an answer.

"We desperately need to figure out what he's planning," was all he could offer.

After notifying the SAC about Joey's illegal entry, Jeannie assembled her team in the briefing room. She brought blown-up pictures of Joey's letter as well an enlargement of his added comments. "OK people, we're up against the proverbial clock. The Time Game is still in Joey's favor; we still don't know what he's planning. We have no location, no time element, nothing. I hope if we put our heads together, or as the progressive's like to say 'worked collaboratively,' we can think this through. I know we can do it. Darcy and Burk decoded Osama bin

Laden's little riddle. We can do it with Joey's letter. Take some time and read, then re-read the letter and his comments from last night. Yes, the son-of-a-bitch reentered my home. Help yourself to refreshments in the back and then we'll start brainstorming. Let's go people!"

Almost on cue, Agent Mathews arrived with donuts, bagels, juice, coffee and tea which Jeannie had requested. Agents helped him place items on the table, with the exception of Darcy and Burk who were more interested in the documents on the wall. Burk took a photo of the document pages and added comments, and downloaded it on a computer that he and Darcy seemed consumed with. Noticing this, Jeannie made up two plates for them, including coffee for Burk and tea for Darcy. "Hey guys, you both need some cop-food for energy," Jeannie said. Both thanked her and returned their attention to the computer screen without touching the food.

After an hour, Jeannie took over the floor. "OK, let's throw out some ideas and see where that takes us."

"I think we may have something to start with," Burk said, standing by the table with the computer. He glanced back at Darcy who was also standing. Walking to the white board, Burk handed one of two dry markers to Darcy. Both focused on the first page of the letters they had projected on the screen, underlining important sentences.

Hello Agent Loomis,

How is my favorite FBI agent? This is Joey. Do you miss me? Jeannie could feel her pulse increase and bile rise in her throat. Sorry for the loss of your fellow agent, Pinheiro. It was never the intention of the Sons and Daughters of Liberty, nor me, to declare war on police. But, like all wars, there will always be collateral damage. I saw you on television and want to congratulate you for being chosen as the task force director on the Koufax serial killing investigation. I hope you are more successful in catching him than you have been in locating me.

"On the first page, we both feel that Joey is bragging about his past accomplishments, both with and without the Sons and Daughters of Liberty. He then tries to pour a little vinegar into your wound, Jeannie, regarding the loss of Agent Pinheiro," Burk said.

"The first paragraph on the second page is a little more interesting," Darcy said moving toward the document on display. The two again underlined parts of the paragraph that intrigued them.

Soon, an event will occur that will have society totally forget all about Mr. Koufax and his infamous deeds. My event will make it in all the history books, although our socialistic education system doesn't teach history so most people will have to hear about it on social media.

While pointing to the comment about Koufax, Darcy said she and Burk felt the deaths caused by the serial killer will dwarf compared to the death toll Joey is anticipating in his attack. "The second thing we underlined, in all the history books, is nothing more than his continued rhetoric about our society.

The bulk of his letter is also just Joey spewing his hatred for our country's current state of affairs as he sees it. He spends a considerable amount of time on this in his letter as you can see," Burk said as he circled the entire diatribe.

I wanted you, Agent Loomis, to be the first person to understand the justification for my action. The United States, America if you will, that I took an oath to defend, is becoming a Marxist state. Every day the radical left chips away at our freedom. If you don't believe me, just look at what is happening in those cities governed by the Democrats. Cities like Los Angeles, San Francisco, Philadelphia, Chicago, Minneapolis, and one of the worst, New York. Even the capital of our U.S. government, Washington D.C., have become testaments to the workings of the Marxist left.

Where MS-13 is gloried by the liberal biased media, as just normal "gang members" who hold jobs and go to school. They downplay the atrocious acts of violence these hoodlums part take in, when in fact, they are an international criminal organization. To me, the last straw was when I heard of a pending bill in Congress called The New Way Forward Act. Are you, Agent Loomis, aware of this bill? Assuming you aren't since you are busy chasing me and Mr. Koufax, I will fill you in. The media, by the way, has given this bill no publicity.

It is sponsored by forty-four House Democrats. It is approximately 4,400 words long, almost exactly the length of the U.S. Constitution. It is designed to create a whole new country. It would remake our immigration system specifically allowing criminals from other countries to move here in complete immunity. I am not exaggerating Agent Loomis. You can look it up after you finish reading my letter.

It is the most radical piece of legislation that has ever been proposed in the history of the United State--ever. Convictions should not lead to deportation. The bill specifically addresses felony convictions, not jaywalking or petty theft--felonies. One representative even bragged about this law breaking the pipeline between prison and deportation, something most Americans are for. Crimes of moral turpitude, such as child molestation, are eliminated, totally, as justification for deportation. The category of aggravated felony is also eliminated under this bill. Bottom line, under this bill no crimes, no matter how grievous, will allow a person to be deported.

If that is not enough, the bill gives judges the right to dismiss deportation requests simply on humanitarian purposes, whatever that means. This will allow anti-

American magistrates, who disagree with deportation, can turn any and all deportation request down simply by saying no, they disagree with the process.

"Then Joey tries to make it personal for you Jeannie, here," Darcy says while underlying the relevant sentence.

Are you mad yet Agent Loomis? *No? This bill states that immigrants desiring to enter the Unites States, who have drug crimes or any moral turpitude charges, including sex with children cannot be used to prevent their entrance into our borders. So, a drug cartel leader is freed from prison in another country, say from Latin America, can waltz right into our country.*

Speak out against this bill, and you are labeled a racist. It would pretty much eliminate ICE since they would be required to go before a magistrate and show that the individual they want to deport is a flight risk, or has a history of violence, but this law prevents them from doing so. If this is not bad enough, this bill changes existing laws to allow rapists, child molesters, and drug dealers at tax paper expense to be brought back into America, by inventing a brand-new right. It is called the Right to Come Home. Can you believe it?

"We feel that it is in this section of the letter that Joey starts hinting about the target," Darcy continued. This whole paragraph lists his disdain for both political parties, but more so for the Democrats.

Most Americans have never heard of this law due to our corrupt Marxist media outlets. Both parties are to blame. The Democrats don't want ma and pa at home to know what they are up to. The Republicans have no balls. They held all three Houses of Congress, yet never went after any of these left-wing radicals. They are all part of the system. A system that is broken. With the Democrats calling the shots, being backed by their cohorts, the press, and the Republicans only spouting hot air, the silent majority is once again, stifled in their pursuit of freedom. That will soon change.

"Here's where we feel we need to direct our focus," said Burk, while Darcy began underlining the appropriate passages.

When you have a malignant tumor, you must cut it out. But if you are too late, the cancer will have already spread, like the situation we are facing as a nation. You cannot just eliminate a few politicians like we did with the judges of the Star Chamber. My message to the silent majority will be loud and clear. Wake up America. Take your nation back.

Glad I got that off my chest and feel so much better knowing that you are now the first to understand the rational or motive for my big event. Again, sorry for your loss, but as Forrest Gump said, shit happens.

"Oh my God. He's going to explode a bomb!" Jeannie shouted. Everyone looked at her and then to each other. No one could come up with another viable alternative. "Somehow, Joey has his hands on another bomb and will use it in his attack?" Jeannie continued.

"Yeah, I agree, but we still don't know the target or date," Ismail said.

"OK people. Think. What big event is nearly upon us that would be a target suitable to Joey's liking?" Jeannie asked, just then SAC Lomax entered the briefing room and heard the tail end of her question.

"The Democratic National Convention is tomorrow in Los Angeles," he said.

CHAPTER 25

After flying back to Los Angeles, Joey spent the day driving around the area. With disgust, he saw more and more evidence that this Democratic managed city had become a third-world country. He saw homeless encampments along freeways and especially under overpasses. Sidewalks were littered with used syringes as well as trash and human waste. Males and females squatted to defecate on the sidewalks while the police just drove by, probably instructed to do so by the mayor.

With still a lot of time in the day, he visited Griffith Park and the observatory located in the eastern hills of the Santa Monica Mountains, providing a great view of the entire city. *Tomorrow evening thousands of liberals will be attending their big convention, having no idea of the panic that will be released upon them,* he thought as he returned to his car.

Agent Mathews dropped Jeannie and Ismail off at the San Francisco International Airport for their short flight to Los Angeles. Meanwhile SAC Lomax contacted the Democrat National Convention security team, the Secret Service, the Los Angeles Police Department, and his counterpart at the Los Angeles FBI bureau. Upon landing, Ismail and Jeannie were picked up by FBI agent Todd Healy, who drove them directly to the auditorium command post. Before leaving, Jeannie discussed the situation with Lomax. Although they were not 100% sure that the convention was the target, no one could offer a more suitable venue for Joey. More importantly, they had no idea how Joey was going to set off the device or devices. If he is in the area and saw an increase in police activity, he might activate the device ahead of time.

The boots on the ground at the arena were told to keep everything low-key so they would not spook Joey. Security was told to continue normal security audits until Jeannie and Ismail arrived.

When they got near the arena, Jeannie instructed Agent Thompson who had driven them from the airport, to radio ahead and let the officials know he would be driving directly inside the auditorium. If Joey were in close proximity and watching the events of the day unfold, recognizing Jeannie at the scene might set him off. Jeannie also requested the command staff to move the media to a position where she could not be photographed. Again, if Joey was watching television somewhere, seeing her could prompt the same result.

"Hello, Agent Loomis, I'm Carl Gray, head of the Democratic National Convention security detail." Jeannie shook his hand and introduced Flores. The others in the room represented LAPD, the Los Angeles Sheriff's Department, the Secret Service Protective service guarding the Democratic nominee, and the FBI. After greetings were concluded, Gray said the NSA would be sending agents as well. The mention of the NSA caused a little stir in Jeannie's chest; it was Ricky Pinheiro's old agency.

All eyes were fixed on Jeannie and Flores. "If you're not aware, in the past this suspect has exploded multiple bombs simultaneously with a cellphone. But during our flight we discussed that this method really would not be effective if, in fact, he plans to set off a virus," Jeannie said. "The heat from a blast would destroy most of the substances' pathogens," Ismail added.

"That makes sense. None of our K-9s alerted to the presence of any bomb making material during our numerous sweeps," LAPD officer Stan McDonald added. "The Secret Service has done how many sweeps already?" he asked. The Secret Service agent said eleven times, and that they would continue to patrol the arena prior to the commencement.

"We believe that he has somehow placed devices in the arena that he can set off remotely once the auditorium is filled to capacity." Just then a uniformed LAPD officer entered the command center and said, "Agent Loomis, the hazmat teams are here."

Joey contemplated visiting either Universal Studios or Disneyland, figuring he had better visit them now, since once the virus was released it would take at least a year before any of the tourist attractions could be visited again. He glanced at his watch. *Who said time flies? It isn't for me,* he thought while trying to decide what to do next. He opted for a quick visit to Farmers Market where he nibbled on a few items offered by the vendors. Next, he visited the California Science Center where he got to see the Space Shuttle Endeavour and The Ecosystems exhibit that featured an impressive 188,000-gallon kelp tank, as well as live plants, animals, and fish. Finally, Joey decided that it was time to head back to the motel room for the eve of the big event.

As a new search was initiated by the Secret Service and other law enforcement agencies, including the Convention security team, Jeannie assembled the rent-a-cops used while construction was going on at the auditorium. She and Ismail showed them pictures of Joey. No one recognized him until Sam Ackerman was interviewed. "Sure, I know him. That's Tommy. He's a cool guy. He knows a lot about sports. We used to have lunch together and shoot the shit. What are you all looking at him for?"

Joey took a cool shower and looked at the take-home pizza and soda laying on the motel bed. *Smells good*, he thought, as he grabbed a can of Coke and popped the top. All the mainstream media channels offered various angles of the upcoming Democratic National Convention taking place the next night. Joey recognized many of the attendees and shouted profanities at the screen, thinking that after one more evening he would not have to tolerate their existence any longer.

He checked his watch and attempted to find a movie that would help him fall asleep, then checked the cellphone on the nightstand. This was a special phone with only one number--the number that would reshape America. With a smile on his face, he took another swig of Coke, turned off the light, and let the voices and music of the movie put him to sleep.

CHAPTER 26

Joey woke up the next morning in a great mood. That evening he would re-write history, or at least cause America to take a steps toward common sense and the America he loved and defended. He checked out of the motel room and found a Denny's down the street on the corner. *I wonder how many Denny's still exist?* he thought. Finding an empty seat at the counter, he placed his order with an older rail-thin woman. Joey could tell she hated her job by her robotic greeting, thinking *Another graduate from our dumbass educational system. Oh well, at least she can make change--I hope.*

The chicken-fried steak, country potatoes, gravy, and sourdough toast were excellent. He read a newspaper that someone had discarded. Once again, the bias news rag had nothing but pictures and descriptions of that night's event and derogatory remarks about the President. This time however, reading the various articles did not upset him as before--probably because he knew he was about to eliminate many of these same reports forever. *Hope you have some reporters there tonight. I would love for them to bring the virus back to your headquarters*, he mused while stirring his third cup of coffee.

He left Denny's and listened to the radio while trying to find the exact exit to take to return his rental and grab a shuttle to the airport. He still had two hours before his flight was scheduled to depart. His plane should touchdown in San Francisco by 8 p.m. where, while sitting in an airport bar, he would place the call. The big call. His connecting flight to Bern, Switzerland would leave at 11 p.m. and take approximately nineteen hours. Of course, he knew there would be no reaction from the crowd inside the arena after he placed his call. The noise would cancel out any sounds from the plungers when they were activated, spraying the lethal virus through the air conditioning ducts and misting onto the unsuspecting liberal crowd.

He knew how deadly the Marburg virus was once an individual became infected. Marburg can spread through human-to-human transmission via direct contact (through broken skin or mucous membranes) with the blood, secretions, organs or other bodily fluids of infected people, and with surfaces and materials (e.g. bedding, clothing) contaminated with the fluids. Attendees would not show immediate signs of being exposed and they would leave the auditorium totally unaware they were all carriers of the deadly disease. *I hope they drink up and become merry*, Joey thought.

Within about three days they will come down with a high fever, severe headache and severe malaise. There would be a period of muscle aches and pains followed by severe watery diarrhea, abdominal pain and cramping, plus nausea and vomiting. The diarrhea can persist for a week. Some of the infected at this phase would show "ghost-like" drawn features, deep-set eyes, expressionless faces and experience extreme lethargy. A non-itchy rash can show up between 2 and 7 days. Within 7 days, it's pretty much over for the poor soul exposed to the virus. They will develop severe hemorrhagic manifestations and experience fatal bleeding, often from multiple areas. Because of severe blood loss, most people die in 8-9 days. With a mortality rate of over 88% without it being weaponized as an aerosol, Joey estimated causalities at near 98%. *Not bad--not bad at all*, he thought.

Sam described the general area where Joey worked. Noticed an electrician coming out of the arena after making an adjustment to the sound equipment, he shouted, "Hey Pete, can you come over here?" Pete walked over and Ismail identified himself and Jeannie. They showed him a picture of Joey which he immediately identified. "Do you remember where Joey was working?" they asked.

"I never got his name," Pete said, "but I sure can show you where he and I worked much of the time. You know don't you, that we had access to the whole building. It's over 720,000 square feet."

"Another drink, sir?" the waitress asked Joey as he watched sports highlights on one of four mounted television sets. "Why not?" he said. He looked at his watch and then heard the first boarding announcement for his flight to San Francisco. He gulped his drink, picked up his carryon and headed for the boarding gate. At first glance, it did not seem like it was going to be a full plane. *Good,* he thought. *Maybe I won't have to sit next to anyone.*

Upon boarding, he found his aisle seat and glanced at his watch. *Almost two-hours left before the misting begins,* he thought with a smile on his face.

"Ladies and gentlemen, this is your captain. We should receive clearance shortly. At this time, please turn off all electronics and make sure your tray is in an upright position. Once we start to taxi, our flight attendants will display an information demonstration about our safety equipment and seatbelt requirements. It appears that we won't be hitting any turbulence on this one hour and twenty-minute flight."

Joey heard the ground crew attach the pushback tractor's towbar to the aircraft. There was a slight jerk and the plane started moving backwards. Joey looked at his watch. *Right on time,* he thought. The flight attendants started down the aisles making sure all passengers had their seatbelts attached and that no electronics were being used. He heard the tow bar being removed, and a few seconds later the captain hit the thrusters lightly, moving the plane forward.

"Ladies and gentlemen, we have been cleared for takeoff. Flight crew, please take your positions."

What a cheap ass airline, Joey thought at not being offered a free beverage or snack. He did not luck out and had to share the row with a slightly overweight individual. Fortunately, he had the aisle seat so he could stretch out his legs. After about 15 minutes in the air, Joey noticed the next passenger wearing a badge with a picture of the Democrat nominee who should be getting ready to make his acceptance speech in the arena.

"Hey," Joey said, deliberately looking at the badge on the passenger's shirt. "I'm surprised you left LA instead of attending the big convention tonight. Tonight's your boy's night isn't it?"

"Hell, I wanted to attend, but I couldn't get tickets. It's a sell-out," came the response.

"A sell-out? Wow, that's great," Joey said with a huge smile on his face that the passenger took as a sign that he, too, was a supporter of the Democratic nominee. Joey visually traced the outline of his fu man chu mustache and asked the passenger if he knew the crowd capacity of the auditorium, even though he knew it by heart. The passenger said he did not know but said there would be thousands of attendees. Joey smiled at his reply.

Everyone's radio came alive in the auditorium with the announcement of "We've found something!"

CHAPTER 27

The flight wasn't unbearable. The guy wearing the nominee's badge slept most of the way to San Francisco, for which Joey was thankful. Checking his watch, he saw that it was now 7:46 p.m. The flight arrived early. *Just enough time to hit the head and get something to eat and drink,* he thought. *Of course, I have a phone call to make.*

He found a Burger King restaurant inside the main terminal and got a Whopper and large order of fries. Instead of eating there, he found a bar close to the departure gate with a vacant three-seat table and sat down. He ordered a dark beer and waited for its arrival which did not take long. The bartender at the other end of the room turned the channel of the flat screen television to CNN. Fuckin CNN. *Those pricks pay all major airports to air their propaganda,* he thought as he unwrapped his burger and dipped a fry into catsup.

"This place is jumping," said the male of the two talking heads handling the event for Fox. "What do you think the nominee is going through right now?" he asked his female co-host. "Well, in my last coverage at the Republican Party Convention, the President was actually watching a baseball game while other dignitaries took turns at the podium listing accolades of the incumbent. I don't think this is happening here tonight. The nominee and his handlers know that he's up against a very, very tough opponent who excels when he's in front of a large audience. Added to this concern is the recent rapid change in the poll numbers now leaning in favor of the President."

They're all fuckin crooks, Joey thought. *Republicans, Democrats--they all share the blame for the what the country's become. Dems more that the GOP, but the blame applies to both parties. That's about to change*, he said to himself as he pulled out the cellphone having only one number in its directory.

He focused on the television screen. *That passenger was right*, he thought. Shots of the arena showed it was packed. *I wonder how many have been paid by the Democrats to attend*, he wondered. *There were a lot of rumors that the nominee couldn't even fill a small restaurant while running for the candidacy. Doesn't matter, it's time. No, I think I'll wait for the nominee to take the podium. For sure, everyone will cram together to hear what the asshole has to say. That's the precise moment I need to send the signal.* He placed his index finger over the send button and waited.

He continued to focus on the screen as he finished his burger and took the last few sips of beer. Finally, after all the bloviation, the Democrat nominee for President walked to the podium. *I wonder if he even knows where he is,* Joey laughed. There were rumors the guy was already showing signs of dementia. *OK, assholes, It's time that I say goodbye.* He looked at the send button and pressed down on it. The signal had been sent. He knew there would no reaction from the crowd. They would continue spouting their left-wing ideology, thinking they would soon be in control and applaud every bullshit talking point the nominee said.

Watching the screen, a big smile appeared on Joey's face. He had changed history with one phone call. At that minute, the deadly mist might even have felt good to those in attendance. Those sitting in the rafters might even have felt droplets if close to the vents, causing them to wipe their brows and faces and furthering the contamination process. He tried to see if any of this appeared on the TV screen, but the cameramen where jumping from shot to shot except when they focused on the most radical left members of the party. Then he saw a shot of the upper deck and saw the air conditioning vent. He could see streams blowing as the air conditioners did their deadly work. He remembered that there was a vent directly overhead where the nominee would be making his acceptance speech. *God, with his age and health problems, he is going to be one of the first to go*, Joey thought. He continued to watch the television broadcast but tuned out both hosts' narrations. He was more intent on watching the crowd, taking personal notes of which lefties were present in the auditorium. As their faces appeared on the screen, Joey kept a running tab in his head--*your dead, your dead, your dead.*

Finally, after lies and more lies by the nominee, Joey had seen enough. The radicals stood on their feet and encouraged everyone around them to stand and shout. Joey felt this was a deliberate effort on their part to show the viewing audience how popular their candidate was versus the rumors, although true, of how he could not draw a crowd to save his ass.

Over the airport speakers he heard the call for the first leg of his trip: the flight to Switzerland via a quick stopover in Munich. Realizing he still had time, he pulled out sleeping pills from his carry-on luggage and headed to the restroom. He decided to take the recommended dose instead of his normal routine of using more than the recommended dosage so he would quickly fall asleep once in the air. *Who knows I might get lucky and sit next to a gorgeous woman*, he thought. Looking a little scraggly, he found an empty sink and pulled out his shaving gear for a quick shave, and bought breath mints at a small convenience store on the way to his gate. He checked out the softcover books but thought it would be a waste of money since he hoped to fall asleep. Glancing at his watch he noted it was almost 10:30; they would be about ready to start boarding. He continued toward the boarding gate and took a seat facing the check-in counter.

Joey never understood why some people pay thousands of dollars to sit in first-class when the plane touches down at the same time for those in coach. He stood up and grabbed his overnight bag when he heard the boarding announcement. Like salmon in a stream, he followed everyone in front of him onto the plane and located his seat. After placing his bag overhead, he took his seat and watched everyone enter the plane, giving a rating for each attractive female.

An extremely overweight lady stopped next to his seat and motioned that she would be occupying the two vacant seats next to him. *So much for having an attractive passenger seating next to me*, he thought. *Oh well, once we're in the air, I'll take more sleeping pills, tell the stewardess not to wake me for meals, and dream of the carnage happening in Los Angeles.*

"Hello, Darcy. Please tell me you found Joey. We did find Jeannie with the help of Homeland Security. Facial recognition had him at LAX this evening. Unfortunately, he's already in the air bound for Switzerland with a long layover in Munich. Sorry."

"Hang on a minute. Fuck, fuck, fuck," Jeannie said as she looked at her watch and Ismail. "Connect me with the SAC, now!" Looking at Ismail, she filled him in. "This prick is as slippery as an eel."

"Yeah, remember what one of the Star Chamber judges said," replied Ismail. "Joey always prides himself of being one step ahead of everyone else. I guess we lost him, and we don't have time to catch up with him."

CHAPTER 28

His flight to Munich wasn't too bad. The behemoth that occupied the two seats beside him stayed in her seats for the most part. He was hungry having skipped at least two meals while sleeping during the flight. He helped his seat mate retrieve her bag from the overhead compartment and watched with a smile as she waddled to the exit. After grabbing his bag, he contemplated what to eat before boarding the Lufthansa flight for the final leg of the trip. He had a very long layover to deal with, but at least he was out of the United States. He opted for a deli sandwich and juice, then hit the restroom before settling at a bar to see if anything had yet broken about his accomplishment. Eventually he made it to the boarding area and found a seat while waiting for his flight to Switzerland. Joey tried to determine the number of attendees that had been infected the previous night, while trying to calculate how many hours had passed in comparison to the time showing on his watch. He also wondered when he would hear news from the fake media networks that a virus had been released at the convention center.

His thoughts were broken when he briefly caught sight in the distance of what appeared to be a captain and flight attendant walking briskly toward the departure gate. *Kind of late, aren't you guys*? he thought. He returned to the book he was reading, and before he knew what was happening, two Glock 9mm weapons were pointed at him.

"Hello, Joey. Did you miss me?" Jeannie asked as Ismail grabbed his right wrist and placed a handcuff on it. Only those seated near Joey noticed what was transpiring. They did not panic nor react. Another male was with Jeannie and Flores dressed in a suit, but not displaying a weapon. Ismail unzipped Joey's jacket, allowing it to drop down over Joey's back and hide the handcuffs.

Joey was in shock and at a loss for words as Jeannie and Ismail began walking him out of the waiting area until three uniformed German police officers took over custody. He was taken to a large detention room located in the basement of the Munich airport where his left cuff was removed by one of the German police officers and re-cuffed onto a ring mounted in the center of the table before him. The officer left him alone in the room with the door shut. Joey saw a window that obviously was a two-way mirror. Jeannie and her partner were probably on the outside looking in, he thought. Five minutes later Jeannie walked in with the unknown male present when he had been taken into custody. Joey had a big smile on his face. He had recovered from what had happened at the airport.

"My favorite FBI agent," he said. "I have to compliment you and your disguise at the airport. I never saw the two of you coming. The way you fill out a stewardess uniform; maybe you should consider a career change. And whom do I have the pleasure of meeting?" he asked while looking at the male.

"Joey, this is Special Agent Delaney of Interpol. I'm out of jurisdiction here, so I arranged for Interpol to give us an assist." Delaney did not say a word, nor did Joey. Both shared a short stare at each other until Joey again focused on Jeannie.

"So, tell me Agent Loomis, how did you track me down?"

"I'm sure you're aware of facial recognition, Joey," Jeannie replied. "We figured you were in the Los Angeles area, so we checked all the major airlines especially those at LAX, and there you were, buying a ticket bound to Switzerland. Initially, time was against us and we weren't able catch up with you until your flight landed here in Germany. Thank God for long layovers, huh? I've never been to Munich. Now, let's start with the preliminaries, shall we? For the record what is your full name?"

"Jeannie, Jeannie. Do you mind if I call you by your first name?" Joey responded.

"Doesn't matter to me, " Jeannie said.

"Great. Let's cut to the chase. You already know my name and horsepower." Joey looked at his watch. "Could you tell me the correct time, Jeannie?" he asked.

"Why, Joey? You're certainly not going anywhere for a long time," Jeannie said with a straight face, glancing at her notepad and then reestablishing eye contact with her nemesis.

"Touché, Agent Loomis."

Jeannie began reading Joey his Miranda Warning with Joey parroting her every word. At the conclusion he indicated that he understood his rights and waived them. He did not want a sleazy attorney anywhere near him.

"Isn't it an irony, Jeannie, that I have been fighting the corrupt system of government of our great nation and those who trash our Constitution, and now I must have those rights in mind in an attempt to save my freedom?"

"Joey, let's cut through the bullshit. You're facing a slew of felonies and will be going to prison for the rest of your life. Your political rhetoric and past deeds will terminate with your incarceration. No one is going to remember you." She hoped that perhaps this would bruise his ego and get him to at least continue his verbal discourse.

"Are you so sure Jeannie?" he asked again looking at his wristwatch. "You still haven't told me if I have the correct time."

"It's almost 8 p.m. in Los Angeles; but a day behind us." As Jeannie said this, she noticed a slight look of panic in Joey's face at the mention of the Southern California city.

"Joey, I don't have all night to play with you, so I'm just going to lay it out for you. But first, I'm going to invite in my partner, Special Agent Ismail Flores, to make sure I cover everything." As Jeannie looked up at the camera in the corner of the interrogation room, Agent Delaney opened the door for Ismail to enter carrying a large paper bag and a laptop. He placed both items on the table and took a seat next to Jeannie, then looked at Joey but did not say anything.

Jeannie opened the bag and took out a plunging device and purposely dropped it on the table in front of Joey. "Jesus," Joey said as he quickly jumped up and ran to the farthest wall in the room.

"Relax. The virus has been removed," Jeannie said.

Joey turned and looked at the device, confirming that the vial of Marburg virus was missing. He looked at both Jeannie and Ismail. "Well played, agents," he said as he returned to his seat. "You know Jeannie, I wasn't impressed with the way you captured Koufax, that serial killer. That buffoon made your job easy for you. It was just that he was a little ahead of your team every time until a tip lead to his arrest. I knew it would be inevitable--that you would catch him. But how did you catch me? I really want to know. I left you no leads."

Jeannie looked at Ismail and both had a smile on their face. "Actually, Joey, you gave us enough clues in the letter you sent me and the notation you made on copies of the letters when you entered my house."

"What clues?" he asked, with a smirk on his face.

Ismail outlined the references Joey made in his letter leading to his arrest. Joey listened intently but did not display any amazement in deducing the ability of Jeannie or her team. "Knowing that you would not be satisfied carrying out your terror on a small scale, we felt the Democratic National Convention would be the prefect stage. We still didn't know what you had planned--maybe a bombing like the way you took out the remaining members of the Star Chamber," Ismail said.

"Do you know a person who's first name is Amir?" Jeannie asked. "He lived in a detached garage in the city of Alameda. Amir was found dead by gunshots in his garage. At first, law enforcement thought they had just a run of the mill homicide to deal with. They searched the garage, and you know what they found? Come on Joey, guess. They found two hidden cameras that also had audio capability. Here, let me show you," she said as she nodded at Ismail.

Ismail opened the laptop and started the video showing Amir greeting Joey in his garage turned residence. "Hey, that looks like you, Joey," Ismail said.

Joey did not show any response on his face. Ismail let the video run long enough so that Joey could hear his discussion of the virus and then see the fatal shooting of Amir. Ismail then closed the laptop which served as a cue for Jeannie to take over.

"Do you know a security guard named Sam?" Jeannie asked. This question caused Joey to stir in his seat and stare at both agents with hatred in his eyes. "Well, Sam remembers you. He called you a cool guy and that you knew a lot about sports. When we questioned him, he even remembered the area you worked in, as well as an electrician that worked nearby. From them, it was pretty easy to find your handy work," Jeannie said, pointing at the empty plunger on the table.

"Our hazmat teams deactivated all three devices and secured the virus. Facial recognition at LAX let us know you intended to fly back to the city by the bay. It was now simply a matter of rushing to get here before your flight to Switzerland departed, although we were prepared to stop the flight if necessary. Flights never leave or arrive on time anyway."

My partner here came up with the idea of dressing as part of the flight crew, and well, you know the rest." When Jeannie wrapped up the connections of all the dots leading to Joey's arrest, Joey began clapping his hands. "Bravo Agent Loomis, Agent Flores. A job well done. But do you realize that your actions will aid in the total collapse of the United States? I heard through the rumor mill that the two of you attended last year's Super Bowl. I therefore assume you both like football." Not waiting for a response, he looked at Jeannie and Ismail.

"In 2012, the NFL had an issue with Tim Tebow kneeling before each game to pray. They also had an issue with Tebow wearing John 3:16 as part of his eye-black to avoid glare, and they made him take it off.

In 2013, the NFL fined Brandon Marshall for wearing green cleats to raise awareness for people with mental health disorders. The following year Robert Griffin III (RG3) entered a post-game press conference wearing a shirt that said, "Know Jesus, Know Peace, but he was forced to turn it inside out by the NFL uniform police before speaking at the podium."

Neither Jeannie nor Ismail interrupted Joey. They allowed him to continue his rant, hoping he might provide more incriminating evidence, although the evidence he faced was already overwhelming.

Joey continued. "In 2015, DeAngelo Williams was fined for wearing "Find the Cure" eye black for breast cancer awareness. In that same year William Gay was fined for wearing purple cleats to raise awareness for domestic violence--not that the NFL has any domestic violence problems. But, in my opinion the most egregious act was when the NFL prevented the Dallas Cowboys from wearing a decal on their helmet in honor of 5 Dallas Police officers killed in the line of duty.

Do you know that the NFL threatened to fine players who wanted to simply wear cleats to commemorate the 15th anniversary of 9/11? You both may say that since the NFL is a private company they can decide what is allowed to be displayed by their players, but in doing so, don't you see that it is another example of Americans losing their rights to free speech and expression?

Sorry, if you do not like my reference to the NFL--since you are both big football fans--but compare those examples to what we see happening in our nation today. The liberal left allows demonstrations in Democratic managed cities to show disrespect for our National Flag, our National Anthem, for America and her people, by mollifying a particular group and its supporters.

And what does the silent majority do? They sit on their asses and do nothing. Oh, they may talk among others who share their disgust, but like sheep, they go along and stay silent. I had a plan to wake up that silent majority, and you two stopped it. Actually, I am not bitter. You're correct Jeannie. I will be in prison for the rest of my life while the nation falls apart; but I will receive three meals a day. I will have free medical, dental, and vision care. My cell will always have free air conditioning and heat in the wintertime. And, from my cell on my private television set, I will watch the nation slide into chaos."

Joey did not fight extradition, and Agent Delaney, through Interpol, arranged for his transport to California to stand trial for numerous crimes.

PROLOGUE

Joey received several life sentences and began his stay at the maximum-security Federal Penitentiary in Atwood, California. He sent a letter to Jeannie spouting off more of his rhetoric, ending the letter with "see you soon." From found documents he had with him at the time of his arrest, numerous federal agencies were able to track down various accounts he had containing profits garnered from various crimes. He would not admit to planning the kidnapping of a young female teenager of a wealthy high-tech firm owner, nor the robbery/murder that he and his assassins performed on a Russian oligarch in San Francisco, but the money found seemed to match his criminal enterprise.

Three weeks after his arrival in what was supposed to be a federal maximum-security prison, Joey was walking outside near the bathroom area. He passed several groups of gang members pumping iron in the yard. The cameras did not pick up what happened, but Joey was later found with seven stab wounds to his chest and neck. His tongue had been cutout and was laying on the ground next to his body. He had a shallow pulse when found, but stopped before medical staff arrived.

A joint terrorism task force working on the Amir homicide were able to successfully track down the lab and lab employee who secured the Marburg virus for Joey. He admitted his participation and demonstrated how he was able to modify the virus into an aerosol delivery system. New security guidelines were put in place in an attempt to prevent something like this from happening again.

Law enforcement did not have an accurate account of the number of individuals Joey or his team of assassins had killed over the course of their criminal enterprise. Jeannie knew that she could link him to the deaths of the magistrates of the secretive Star Chamber court which would include the bombing that took out the remaining members. No one knew how many executions they performed for the clandestine court since no records were ever found. And it was Joey and his cohorts who killed her fiancé, Rickey Pinheiro. For Joey, his time had run out. He lost the time game.

Back at her residence, Jeannie hired a painter and crew to finish painting the inside of her home. She asked that they use up the leftover paint Ricky had been using, and clean up the whole area upon completion. Jeannie bought a swim spa for her backyard which included a large cedar gazebo enclosure. *Sorry Delores,* she thought as it was being erected. *Ricky and I don't want you to have a heart attack if I'm ever in the heat of passion with someone.*

She ran into Delores on several occasions after closing the case on Joey and was shocked to learn that Delores and husband Walter had taken several firearms courses. *God help us,* Jeannie thought. "I bet you're laughing up there in heaven, aren't you Ricky," she said while considering what she wanted to take to her cabin in Idaho. She was looking forward to finishing her audio book, "*Hitting Rock Bottom*" on the trip north. The stories told by young juvenile delinquents, now called cadets, who attended a military boot camp school made her laugh, cry, and think.

The November Presidential election resulted in a landslide win for the incumbent. A few months later, the Democratic nominee died from the Covid-19 virus. The joke going around was that he wasn't even aware he was running for anything.

Look for Gary J. Rose's next Jeannie Loomis novel

THIN BLUE LINE

sneak preview follows ....

In San Francisco, crime had become epidemic. Gangs fought over drug turf leaving corpses in their wake. The San Francisco Police Department was overwhelmed as the homicide rate climbed.

Before officers could stem the tide of violence, they became the targets. A cop killer was on the loose and police turned to the FBI.

CHAPTER ONE

Officer Ronnie Grayson liked his part-time job at Donuts and Mud, the Millennial version of the once national chain, Winchell's Donuts. He remembers fondly when his dad shared cop-talk, or what they called wargames, with fellow officers who would stop by after his retirement to shoot the shit. Now retired after a thirty-year career on the force, he was paying the price for eating all those donuts over the years, and recently underwent a quadruple bypass.

Grayson followed in his shoes and chose a career in law enforcement, joining the SFPD four and a half years ago. He took the part-time security guard job at the donut shop because he needed money as a part-time law school student. The department allowed him to wear his SFPD uniform while on the job, hoping it would discourage robberies. It had become common practice to allow uniformed officers to moonlight as security officers, especially during the recent crime escalation. Businesses, customers, and employees alike felt more secure with their presence.

Today he sat in his customary seat, a booth facing the entrance to the shop. Studying the subject of Torts on his laptop, he did not notice the African American walk up to the front glass façade. No one inside saw the dark figure of a person firing three rapid shots into the establishment until they saw him move and disappear into the darkness and fog that had descended onto San Francisco's streets. Two bullets grazed the back of Grayson's neck.

He peered into the darkness to see if he could see the shooter, then radioed for assistance. He did not know the direction the shots came from or if the gunman was still out there waiting to take another shot.

Responding officers raced to the scene, but the gunman was nowhere in sight. There was no robbery attempt; it appeared that the sole purpose was to kill the officer where he was seated.

Based on witness accounts, the police felt the shooter acted alone. The forensic team found three 9mm shell casings outside on the sidewalk, and slugs found in the donut shop walls confirmed that they came from a semi-automatic.

Although Officer Grayson survived the shooting with only minor injuries, other officers later targeted by the gunman would not be so lucky.

Less than three weeks later, a hooded figure entered a bar frequented by law enforcement officers. Before the officers could react, five rounds were fired. In an instant, three individuals were hit. One was a police sergeant; the other two were federal agents. All three died. Again, the shooter was swallowed by the San Francisco fog and disappeared.

Sometime during the night, Jeannie in a half-awake, half-dream state thought about her life.

Her self-examination concluded that she was a mid-forty female, not bad-looking--if she could brag to herself--divorced twice, childless, and the Assistant Special Agent in Charge with the Federal Bureau of Investigation in San Francisco. Currently not dating and still coping with the loss of her fiancé Ricky killed by urban terrorists, Jeannie felt that things could only get better going forward.

Jeannie woke to the ringtone of her cellphone. Before answering, she looked at her alarm clock. It was 1:18 a.m. No one can expect good news from a call at that hour. It had to be the bureau. "Loomis," she said waiting for the bad news. Sure enough, she was informed that three officers had been fatally shot at a cop bar in the "City by the Bay's" Mission District. One was an FBI agent that reported to Jeannie; the others were federal agents working for the U.S. Department of Fish and Wildlife.

Initially, she could not put a face to the FBI agent's name since several agents had been transferred in recently due to the bureaucratic FBI's shake-up in D.C. House cleaning was still underway from the corruption fallout at the top of the bureau. Fortunately for Jeannie, she was able to stay under the radar and continued her climb up the promotion ladder. The agent's name was Michael Atwood, a 32 years old husband and father-to-be.

She requested dispatch to notify her partner Special Agent Ismail Flores and have him meet her at the bar. When possible, Jeannie visited crime scenes to take in the environment, smells, and anything else that might help her analyzing her gut feelings which she felt most successful officers use to solve crimes.

Jeannie Loomis was a seventeen-year veteran of the FBI, rapidly climbing the ranks which had previously been male-heavy at the top. After surviving a shooting in one of their satellite offices, she was offered the SAC job in San Francisco, but opted to take the Assistant position to learn the ropes. She was successful in arranging the transfer of her co-worker, friend, and confidant, Special Agent Ismail Flores, and two topnotch IT specialists, Darcy and Burk.

She and her team had recently solved an armored car robbery turned homicide case, taking down four suspects. After Jeannie took over the director reins of a serial killer task force, she and her team successfully captured the elusive Daniel Koufax. However, all of these investigations took a backseat to their case involving the notorious Joey, former leader of the Sons and Daughters of Liberty. This assassination squad eliminated individuals found guilty by the secret Star Chamber. Joey had placed canisters of the deadly Marburg virus in the air conditioning ducts at the Los Angeles convention center hoping to infect attendees of the Democratic National Convention. Acting in time, Jeannie and her team removed the deadly virus and took Joey into custody as he was leaving the United States. He later died at the hands of fellow inmates.

The Elbow Room Bar located at 647 Valencia Street was initially home to the city's landmark lesbian bar, Amelia's, which was open in the 1970s and 1980s. The building is a two-story structure with the main bar downstairs; a secondary bar adjoins the dance floor and stage upstairs. The club caters to a wide range of musical tastes.

On any given night, live bands and DJs play rock, hip-hop, soul, metal, indie, and a little punk. Most cops hangout on the first floor--the floor where the shootings took place.

Jeannie parked her Vette near the taped off area behind Ismail's bureau Crown Vic. "Hey, Ace," she said as she saw Ismail near the entrance. "How bad is it?"

"It's not a drive-by. This cold-blooded motherfucker walked into the bar and fired off at least five or more rounds, and then walked out. It was a deliberate attack," Ismail said.

"My gut tells me that it won't be this guy's last."

"Any idea who the target was?" Jeannie asked.

"Too early to tell, but I guess we can't rule out anything at this point. It could be just many cops trying to release some stress after work, a random shooting, or one of those hit was the target, and the others were just collateral damage. Who knows?" Ismail replied.

"OK, I've already requested that our Chaplin meet me at Atwood's home in Oakland. You stay here while forensic does their thing and see if we have any more to work with. After I meet with Atwood's wife, I'll meet you at the bureau and we can review everything," Jeannie said as she started walking to her vehicle, dreading what might lie ahead when she makes the death notification.

"Don't envy you, boss," said Ismail. "Sure you don't want me to tag along?"

"No, thanks for the offer; the Chaplin and I should have it under control. If you feel a need for more manpower, go ahead and call them in. The media will be all over it by tomorrow morning.

CHAPTER TWO

To Jeannie, the drive to Oakland seemed to take forever. She didn't remember the drive across the Oakland-San Francisco Bay Bridge or the climb up the foothills overlooking the city. There was nothing Jeannie liked about Oakland: high crime rate and homeless encampments everywhere. It seemed to be a mirror of San Francisco without the views. She remembered something that Joey, the now-dead urban terrorists of the Sons and Daughters of Liberty, said while she and her team pursued the elusive mastermind. "One thing all these cities have in common," he said, "was that they were all managed by Democrats."

Trying to keep her mind from the task before her, Jeannie had to agree with Joey. Think of all the cities now under duress--riots, fires, mayhem, shootings, murder in Philadelphia, Chicago, Minneapolis, San

Francisco, Los Angeles, Portland, Seattle, and on-and-on--all managed by a Democratic mayor or governor, or both.

She had no problem finding the address. It was a nice home for the neighborhood; she wondered how one of her agents could afford such a residence.

I need to investigate this later, she thought. As she prepared to get out of her car, she received a text saying that the Chaplain had also just arrived. She saw parking lights reflect off of another parked car and saw the Chaplain exit her vehicle. Getting out of her Ford Mustang, Shelly Wilcox saw Jeannie, waved and walked toward her. "Sorry for your loss," Shelly said.

"Thanks, but to be honest with you, he was a new transfer so I don't know anything about him. I'm so glad you were free to meet me here. I hate these things, but more so when I don't feel I have anything to contribute," Jeannie replied.

"I understand completely. If you introduce yourself and me, and explain what happened I can take over. Most of the death notices I have to make are about individuals I don't know. I hate to say it, but we have a well-rehearsed narrative that all of us Chaplains use to accomplish our task. The main thing we all have to avoid is coming across like a robot."

The house was dark, but the exterior had outdoor lighting. Jeannie rang the doorbell and she and Shelly waited for several minutes. At first, they thought that perhaps no one was at home, but finally they heard footsteps coming toward the front door and the porch light illuminated. Jeannie could see movement behind the door's peephole followed by a female voice saying hello. Jeannie took a deep breath and identified herself, raising her identification to the peephole.

"Oh my God," she screamed. "Is Mike alright?" she asked while removing a security chain and unlocking the door. Mrs. Atwood was wearing a bathrobe that did little to conceal her pregnancy. Her hair showed that she had been sleeping. "It's about Mike. Is he alright?" she asked again. Jeannie requested that she and Shelly enter the residence. Once instead, but before sitting, Jeannie formally introduced herself.

"Your Mike's supervisor, right?" she asked.

"Yes, and this is Shelly Wilcox." Jeannie did not identify Wilcox as a Chaplain. Mrs. Atwood, maybe we should all sit down."

"Yes, yes. I'm sorry, please have a seat," Mrs. Atwood said while pointing to a couch. Please, call me Marsha."

"Marsha," Jeannie said. "There was a shooting tonight at a bar in San Francisco. Three individuals were shot, and one was your husband."

Marsha began to cry and placed her hand over her unborn child. "I'm so sorry. Mike did not make it."

"No. You have to be wrong. Mike and I are having a baby. He can't be dead. I think you have him mixed up with someone else. Mike promised he would always wear a bullet-proof vest. No. Mike is fine. He called me and told me he would have a drink with Rob at some bar in the city. Rob works undercover for the Federal Fish and Wildlife Department. Rob would have called me if Mike got hurt."

At this point, the Chaplin took over. Jeannie could not recall on her drive back across the bay if Shelly eventually identified her position or not.

Jeannie began having flashbacks of being notified by the surgeon of her fiancé Ricky Pinheiro's death. She caught herself tearing up and had to wipe her eyes with the cuff of her long-sleeved blouse. She loved her job except for moments like these, but fortunately for her they were few and far between. Even though the SFPD was being crushed with an overwhelming increase in violent crimes, including one homicide a day, they had not affected the bureau per se until now. It was about to get even worse.

Jeannie arrived at her office at the same time SAC (Special Agent in Charge) Lomax was leaving the breakroom. "Heard you had an early morning," he said while carrying a cup of coffee. "How was the death notification?" he asked not wanting an answer, having done many himself over his career.

"Thank God Shelly Wilcox was on-call. She carried most of the burden. What hurt me the most was that I never really met Michael. I was so tied up with the serial killer task force and then with the armored car robbery that I never had time to sit down and talk with him. Hell, I never even looked at his file," Jeannie said while unlocking her office door and entering.

Lomax took a seat opposite Jeannie. Neither person said anything at first. "Look, for what it's worth, I did have a chance to have a coffee with Michael after transferring here. He was part of the house cleaning effort conducted by Washington. He confided in me that he was so glad to get transferred out of D.C. and relocated to the bay area with his pregnant wife. He called D.C. a cesspool, and I couldn't agree more. He said that the bureau's higher ranks were so corrupt with hatred for the President that he almost left the bureau out of disgust. Did you know his great-grandfather was an agent under J. Edgar Hoover, himself, back in the Al Capone era? Listened to all the stories his grandfather relived created his desire to wear the badge."

Agent Ismail Flores, Jeannie's senior agent, saw Lomax sitting across from her and knocked before entering. "If I'm interrupting..." he said, but Lomax stood, patted Ismail and the shoulder before receiving an answer and left Jeannie's office. "Tough day for everyone around here, huh!" he commented. "That's an understatement. So, what do we have on the shootings?"

"Appears to have been a single shooter. We found numerous 9mm shell casings. A preliminary review by forensics shows no prints. Looks like he fired ten rounds--one whole clip. According to witnesses, he entered the bottom floor bar area, already with the gun in his hand. He didn't walk too far inside. Looking at no one in particular, he opened fire until he ran out of bullets, then turned and left. Cool, calm, and collected. Could be a pro, but since he didn't seem focused on one particular person--I don't know. Maybe he's ex-military."

"Any surveillance tapes?" Jeannie asked.

"Only from outside the bar, but with the fog--they're worthless. I already gave them to Darcy and Burk to see if they could be cleaned up, but I doubt it. This is going to be a who-done-it," Ismail replied.

CHAPTER THREE

Three days later at 2:15 p.m., only six blocks from the SFPD Richmond Station, officer Matt Riley, a 26-year old and 6-year veteran of the force, was writing up a report inside his patrol vehicle. Using his dash-mounted lamp, he was quickly checking all the boxes on his computer to file his report, hoping his sergeant would not kick it back later.

Usually, he would have just kissed off the incident as a family fight with no one wanting to press charges; but nowadays, with all the domestic violence crap he needed to cover his ass with a report. A taxicab was double-parked on the opposite side of the street. Officer Riley looked at the cab but did not see anyone enter or exit, nor was it illuminated. He continued working on his report.

He didn't hear a man approach his cruiser. The man raised his hand and fired four times into Riley's body at close range, hitting the chest, stomach, and shoulder. Riley was able to struggle out of his patrol car and fire off two rounds at the fleeing male suspect before falling to his knees, and then face-first to the ground.

The cab driver, Mamood Abass, witnessed the shooting and quickly contacted his dispatcher, describing the suspect's escape route. Remaining on the line with his dispatcher, he circled the block to see if he could track the shooter.

As the gunman ran through the alleyway, he discarding his hoodie and black ski mask to change his appearance. Turning the corner at the next block, the cabbie saw the alley's shooter emerge. "I got him. I got him," he said to his dispatcher as the shooter was hailing the cab to stop. Before stopping, he told his dispatcher that the shooter was a lift.

Not realizing the cabbie had witnessed the shooting and before the driver could react, the assailant climbed into the cab's back seat. The cabbie discreetly turned off his radio. Focusing on the black male now seating in his cab, he quickly assumed various positions as if looking to see if he was being followed. He noted that the gunman was wearing black leather gloves that exposed half of his fingers, while his right hand held a semi-automatic. Simultaneously, the dispatcher was contacting the SFPD. The shooter did not give the driver a final destination, only telling him to drive straight or make turns.

SFPD put out a BOLO (be on the lookout) for cab number 662, which was also being tracked by an onboard GPS tracking device. The driver tried to remain calm, knowing the police were trying to find his cab behind the scenes. Within minutes, SFPD Officer Stan Alshire pulled behind the cab. The shooter saw the patrol unit and placed his gun against Mamood's head, barking out an address. Another patrol unit joined the first. Mamood made a right turn and suddenly slammed on the breaks.

The gunman, startled by the abrupt stop, kicked open the back door, bolted out of the cab, dropped his weapon on the ground, and flew into the neighborhood, evading the pursuing officers. The officers retrieved the weapon which held six 9 mm bullets--four less than a fully-loaded clip. Backup officers searched the area, but the gunman had disappeared.

At the crime scene Officer Riley was fighting for his life. He was placed on a gurney and rushed to the hospital. Remarkably, he survived emergency surgery that removed four bullets from his body. Forensic team members in the alley photographed the entire area before tagging and bagging the hoodie and black ski mask discarded by the shooter.

Jeannie was lost in thought at her desk when her phone rang. It was SAC Lomax.

"Jeannie, there's been another cop shooting in the city. I don't know if there's any connection to the bar shooting, but I told SFPD we'd send someone over to see what they have and compare notes. If you and Ismail are free, I'd like to run over there."

Jeannie rode with Ismail to the Richmond Station, getting directions to the first crime scene where Officer Riley had been shot. The forensic team assigned to this location was just finishing up. Detective Tom Hanson saw the two agents identify themselves to the officer behind the crime scene tape and approached them. After shaking hands, he told Jeannie and Ismail what they already surmised.

Not getting much from that location, they headed to crime scene number two after Detective Hanson described the route they needed to take. The forensic team that had been there had already left, but two uniformed officers remained.

"Male, black. About 25-30 years old. 5'9" to 6'1." Average build. Clean shaven. Short hair. Calm and cool according to the cabbie," Officer Sally Yates said while her partner, Sam Prescot listened. "He probably jumped several fences and was out of here before we could conduct a thorough search. Couldn't use the chopper due to the fog. No one saw or heard anything, or they don't want to get involved," she added.

Upon Jeannie's return to the bureau, her receptionist told her the SAC wanted to see her when she got back. Ismail said he was heading to the breakroom and that the two of them could meet up later.

Jeannie picked up her While-U-Out messages and walked down the hallway to Lomax's office. She found him talking on the phone, sitting with his back to the entrance door. From what she overhead, she surmised he was talking to a higher-up with the San Jose Police Department, but he concluded the call before she could speculate its nature.

"I know you want to hunt for your cop killer, but you've been requested by Washington to assist the San Jose Police Department on a serial killer case they may have. I guess your behavior analysis skills are known throughout this wacko state we call California. Before you object, let me tell you what they have up to this point." Jeannie took a deep breath and put her messages on Lomax's desk.

"I just got off the phone with Captain Williams of the San Jose Police Department. They have a vicious killer on the loose in the southern part of the city who's heading down to Morgan Hill and Gilroy. His hunting grounds appear to be the rural, undeveloped areas still down there. This son-of-a-bitch preys on the elderly and the weak.

His M.O. (modus operandi) appears to be gaining entrance into their homes and attacking them as they sleep. After his third kill, they realized they had a serial killer on their hands. Not making any headway on their own, they contacted our BAU (Behavioral Analysis Unit) in Quantico who provided their perspective of his behavior and possible motivation. Nevertheless, Bill, Captain Williams, has heard about your role as task force director in the Marin County serial and he's requesting your help."

Jeannie knew that Lomax was not a fan of whining, so she did not object to aiding the SJPD. "OK, I can leave Ismail and the team to work on our case. Do you have Captain William's phone number? I'll give him a call? It's not like television, is it?" she asked.

"What do you mean?" he asked.

"In a television show the whole God damn BAU would jump in a private jet and fly out to the requesting agency."

"I see what you mean. Sadly, here we put our best agent in a red Corvette and send her on her way. Good luck; make me proud."

CHAPTER FOUR

"Hey Ace, I'm afraid I must leave you in charge again. San Jose P.D. feels they have a serial killer, and they've requested our assistance," Jeannie said.

"Gee, I'm telling you ladies and gentlemen, we have a celebrity right here in our midst," Ismail said as he was finishing his coffee and suppressing a laugh.

"Hilarious, asshole," she responded. "Don't mess up my office while I'm gone--and no, you can't keep my car. It's not a perk that goes with the job."

"Bummer. I was hoping of taking the wifey for a spin and maybe getting lucky afterward."

"You know, that could be perceived as sexual harassment or something in our politically correct society today."

"No, my wife loves it. I'm the one being harassed. She can't keep her hands off me."

"Right. You need to see the shrink and get that narcissistic personality disorder checked," she said while laughing. I'll give you a check-in call tonight to see how your case is going and get an update on the latest in San Jose."

After calling Captain Williams and setting up a time later that afternoon to meet, Jeannie headed for home to pack an overnight bag in case she had to stay in the south-bay city longer than expected. San Jose is California's third-largest city, only beaten out by Los Angeles and San Diego. It is surrounded by the rolling hills of Silicon Valley and San Francisco Bay's southern shore to the north, and it is the major technology hub of the Bay Area. Its population hovers around 1.1 million, but swells with employees commuting into the area during the workweek to perform high-tech jobs. Besides being located within a booming high-tech industry area, San Jose is a cultural, political, and economic center, earning the city's nickname "Capital of Silicon Valley." Major global tech companies including Cisco Systems, eBay, Adobe Inc, PayPal, Broadcom, Samsung, Acer, Hewlett Packard, and Zoom, maintain their headquarters in San Jose.

Living in San Jose is not much cheaper than the rest of the bay area, although the farther south one goes, the more affordable things become. Jeannie knew that the average home was over $1 million, and for that you get a home manufactured in the 1950s during the baby boom. It has the fifth most expensive housing market in the world.

Jeannie's long deceased dad used to discuss the transformation of San Jose on their extended family drives down to Watsonville, farther south on the coast. San Jose was initially divided into a downtown area, and the central and western parts. As the population grew, people began referring to North, South, East, and West San Jose areas. Many of these regions were originally unincorporated communities or separate municipalities that were later annexed by the city. Like all large cities, there were good areas and areas to avoid if possible.

Jeannie was very familiar with the area, having driven many times by herself when she got older or with friends. She knew the city itself covered over 180 square miles, so the killers hunting ground was huge. She had also visited the famed Winchester Mystery House several times, not to be amused by the tour guides' tales about the "haunted house" and its ghostly inhabitants, but to admire the house's craftsmanship and construction.

In the 1970s, Whites made up over 98% of the population, but that fell in the 21st century to only 42%. Now, almost 60% of the population is comprised of Hispanics and Asians, with only 3% Black. *It will be interesting to see if the San Jose Police Department has any witnesses who could give us the perps nationality*, Jeannie thought as she navigated through the traffic on Highway 101. Finally, she arrived at 121

West Mission Street, the San Jose Police Department. She parked her bureau car on the street and fed the parking meter. In San Francisco she could leave her Vette in the bureau's secured garage.

She knew the PD has almost one-thousand officers; however, still less than the San Francisco PD. Having never had contact with Captain Williams, she knew a few detectives at the department from when she taught a Behavioral Analysis class at the Evergreen College campus. She found them very professional and highly trained. With that in mind, she wondered why she had been requested. Certainly, they had the collective experience in the department to track down this killer.

She showed her ID at the front counter and told the duty officer that Captain Williams was expecting her. After taking a seat, and before she had the opportunity to make her way through a stack of old magazines, she heard a buzz and Williams appeared. "Agent Loomis, I'm glad to meet you," he said, while offering his hand. After greetings were exchanged, Williams invited Jeannie to follow him to his office. "How was the drive down from the city? I have to tell you, I hate driving up the 101 to SF these days. When I was a kid, it was always a thrill to see Alcatraz, the bridges, and the Painted Ladies. At least I think that's what those old houses are called."

"You're right. They're called the Painted Ladies. Have you ever gone inside one of them on a tour?" Jeannie asked. "No, and like I said, I try to avoid the

City-by-the-Bay at all costs. It's sad to see what the city has become. No offense."

"None taken," Jeannie responded. "Most of the agents I work with feel the same way."

While walking to his office, they stopped at the breakroom where Jeannie was offered coffee. She turned that down, but asked for directions to the restrooms. Williams was waiting when she returned, and they continued to his large office.

"Jeannie, this is the most brutal, cold-blooded killer I have ever investigated, and I'm going on 30 years on the force. He's not satisfied with just killing individuals--each act is an act of overkill. It's as if he goes into a frenzy after the victim is already dead. The fact that most of his victims are elderly and frail doesn't seem to affect the bastard at all. He's a cold-blooded sociopath. He doesn't take a backseat to Richard Ramirez, the Night Stalker, you know--in the mid-80s. I think when we meet with the other detectives and they tell you what we have, you'll note a lot of similarities to that case."

www.ingramcontent.com/pod-product-compliance
Lightning Source LLC
Chambersburg PA
CBHW020552310726
48979CB00008B/1183/J

* 9 7 8 1 7 3 4 8 5 2 4 3 1 *